BUFFALO TALES

OF THE
NATIVE AMERICAN INDIANS

Written and Edited by G.W. Mullins
With Original Art by C.L. Hause

Light Of The Moon Publishing

© 2023 by G.W. Mullins and C. L. Hause

ISBN: 978-1-958221-15-0

First Edition Printing

Light Of The Moon Publishing has allowed this work to remain exactly as the author intended, verbatim, without editorial input.

Printed in the United States of America

The following book represents a collection of Native American works which are public domain. You may have read the stories before. In true story telling fashion, the stories have been left as close to the original form as possible. In Native American culture, in order to pass the stories along with all information intact, they had to be told pretty much word for word, to keep the legends alive. Many of these stories were translated directly from original Native language texts. With that in mind, please be aware that some spellings and word usage may vary from one tribe to another. For instance, the spelling of "teepee", as used in this book, can also be written as "tipi", and "tepee". All are correct. Also, when using words like "someone", in most native cultures, it would be "some one". So, keep in mind, these are not necessarily misspellings. They are simply dialect and translations.

This book is dedicated to Vince Mullins, my Grandfather (Pawpaw). He was a tall red man with fire in his eyes… who I loved so much.

This book is also dedicated to one of my heroes, Chief Dan George, a true visionary.

G.W. Mullins

Chief Dan George, (July 24, 1899 – September 23, 1981) was a chief of the Tsleil-Waututh Nation, a Coast Salish band located on Burrard Inlet in North Vancouver, British Columbia, Canada. He was also an author, poet, actor, and an Officer of the Order of Canada. At the age of 71, he was nominated for an Academy Award for Best Supporting Actor in Little Big Man.

What is life? It is the flash of a firefly in the night. It is the breath of a buffalo in the wintertime. It is the little shadow which runs across the grass and loses itself in the sunset.

– Blackfoot

Also Available From G.W. Mullins And C.L. Hause

Star People, Sky Gods And Other Tales Of The Native American Indians

Coyote Tales Of The Native American Indians

Bear Tales Of The Native American Indians

More Star People, Sky Gods And Other Paranormal Tales Of The Native American Indians

Walking With Spirits Native American Myths, Legends, And Folklore Volumes One Thru Six

The Native American Cookbook

Native American Cooking - An Indian Cookbook With Legends And Folklore

The Native American Story Book - Stories Of The American Indians For Children Volumes One Thru Five

The Best Native American Stories For Children

Cherokee A Collection of American Indian Legends, Stories And Fables

Creation Myths - Tales Of The Native American Indians

Strange Tales Of The Native American Indians

Spirit Quest - Stories Of The Native American Indians

Animal Tales Of The Native American Indians

Medicine Man - Shamanism, Natural Healing, Remedies And Stories Of The Native American Indians

Native American Legends: Stories Of The Hopi Indians Volumes 1 and 2

Totem Animals Of The Native Americans

The Best Native American Myths, Legends And Folklore Volumes 1 Thru 3

Ghosts, Spirits And The Afterlife In Native American Indian Mythology And Folklore

The Native American Art Book – Art Inspired By Native American Myths And Legends

Animal Tales Of The native American Indians Vol. 2

Origin Tales Of The Native American Indians

THE NATIVE AMERICAN STORY COLLECTION SERIES
Featuring The Writing Of Best-Selling Author
G.W. MULLINS
And Original Art From
Award Winning Artist C.L. HAUSE
The Native American Story Book Series / The Best Native American Stories For Children
Tales Of The Native American Indians / Native American Legends Series
Animal Tales Of The Native American Indians
Creation Myths Tales Of The Native American Indians
Cherokee
Native American Cooking, Art And Medicine Books
Native American Cooking
THE NATIVE AMERICAN ART BOOK
C.L. HAUSE
Walking With Spirits Native American Myths, Legends, And Folklore Series
WALKING WITH SPIRITS
The Best Native American Myths, Legends And Folklore / Supernatural Tales
Best Native American
Ghosts, Spirits, and the Afterlife
Supernatural
LIGHT OF THE MOON PUBLISHING

The American Indian is of the soil, whether it be the region of forests, plains, pueblos, or mesas. He fits into the landscape, for the hand that fashioned the continent also fashioned the man for his surroundings. He once grew as naturally as the wild sunflowers; he belongs just as the buffalo belonged....

– Luther Standing Bear, Oglala Sioux Chief

Lakota Instructions for Living

Friend do it this way - that is,
whatever you do in life,
do the very best you can
with both your heart and mind.

And if you do it that way,
the Power Of The Universe
will come to your assistance,
if your heart and mind are in Unity.

When one sits in the Hoop Of The People,
one must be responsible because
All of Creation is related.
And the hurt of one is the hurt of all.
And the honor of one is the honor of all.
And whatever we do affects everything in the
universe.

If you do it that way - that is,
if you truly join your heart and mind
as One - whatever you ask for,
that's the Way It's Going To Be.

Passed down from White Buffalo Calf Woman

Table of Contents

Introduction

Native American Mythology began long before the European settlers arrived on North American soil. Contrary to popular beliefs, there is more to Native American Folklore than stories of buffalo hunts, teepee living and animal stories. Hundreds of tribes throughout North American created a huge mythological system that has rivaled that of the Greeks. Many of these tales have been lost, or are often hard to find. This collection represents a history that should be remembered.

As a Native American myself, I embrace these stories. Native Americans tribes offer such a rich heritage. They have recorded a huge amount of their history through storytelling. In these stories you will relive their history and the lives of North America's First People.

The stories in this book have been handed down from generation to generation. And in such tradition, they are now handed down to you, to share with the next generation.

Included in this anthology, are a group of collected works from the well-known, to the often-forgotten tribes. The tales included within this book, feature some of the most familiar and popular recorded… the stories if the Buffalo.

Song of the Buffalo

An American Indian Legend - Nation Unknown

When the Buffalo first came to be upon the land, they were not friendly to the people. When the hunters tried to coax them over the cliffs for the good of the villages, they were reluctant to offer themselves up. They did not relish being turned into blankets and dried flesh for winter rations. They did not want their hooves and horn to become tools and utensils nor did they welcome their sinew being used for sewing. "No, no," they said. We won't fall into your traps. And we will not fall for your tricks." So, when the hunters guided them towards the abyss, they would always turn aside at the very last moment. With this lack of cooperation, it seemed the villagers would be hungry and cold and ragged all winter long.

Now one of the hunters had a daughter who was very proud of her father's skill with the bow. During the fullness of summer, he always brought her the best of hides to dress, and she in turn would work the deerskins into the softest, whitest of garments for him to wear. Her own dresses were like the down of a snow goose, and the moccasins she made for the children and the grandmothers in the village were the most welcome of gifts.

But now with the hint of snow on the wind, and deer becoming more scarce in the willow breaks, she could see this reluctance on the part of the Buffalo families could become a real problem.

Hunter's Daughter decided she would do something about it. She went to the base of the cliff and looked up. She began to sing in a low, soft voice, "Oh, Buffalo family, come down and visit me. If you come down and feed my relatives in a wedding feast, I will join your family as the bride of your strongest warrior."

She stopped and listened. She thought she heard the slight rumbling sound of thunder in the distance. Again, she sang, "Oh, Buffalo family, come down and visit me. Feed my family in a wedding feast so that I may be a bride."

The thunder was much louder now. Suddenly the Buffalo family began falling from the sky at her feet. One very large bull landed on top of the others, and walked across the backs of his relatives to stand before Hunter's Daughter.

"I am here to claim you as my bride," said Large Buffalo.

"Oh, but now I am afraid to go with you," said Hunter's Daughter.

"Ah, but you must," said Large Buffalo, "For my people have come to provide your people with a wedding feast. As you can see, they have offered themselves up."

"Yes, but I must run and tell my relatives the good news," said Hunter's Daughter. "No," said the Large Buffalo. No word need be sent. You are not getting away so easily."

And that with said, Large Buffalo lifted her between his horns and carried her off to his village in the rolling grass hills.

The next morning the whole village was out looking for Hunter's Daughter. When they found the mound of Buffalo below the cliff, the father, who was in fact a fine tracker as well as a skilled hunter, looked at his daughter's footprints in the dust.

"She's gone off with a Buffalo, he said. I shall follow them and bring her back."

So, Hunter walked out upon the plains, with only his bow and arrows as companions. He walked and walked a great distance until he was so tired that he had to sit down to rest beside a Buffalo wallow.

Along came Magpie and sat down beside him. Hunter spoke to Magpie in a respectful tone, "O knowledgeable bird, has my daughter been stolen from me by a Buffalo? Have you seen them? Can you tell me where they have gone?"

Magpie replied with understanding, "Yes, I have seen them pass this way. They are resting just over this hill."

"Well," said Hunter, would you kindly take my daughter a message for me? Will you tell her I am here just over the hill?"

So, Magpie flew to where Large Buffalo lay asleep amidst his relatives in the dry prairie grass. He hopped over to where Hunter's Daughter was quilling moccasins, as she sat dutifully beside her sleeping husband. "Your father is waiting for you on the other side of the hill," whispered Magpie to the maiden.

"Oh, this is very dangerous," she told him. These Buffalo are not friendly to us and they might try to hurt my father if he should come this way. Please tell him to wait for me and I will try to slip away to see him."

Just then her husband, Large Buffalo, awoke and took off his horn. "Go bring me a drink from the wallow just over this hill," said her husband.

So, she took the horn in her hand and walked very casually over the hill. Her father motioned silently for her to come with him, as he bent into a low crouch in the grass. "No," she whispered. The Buffalo are angry with our people who have killed their people. They will run after us and trample us into the dirt. I will go back and see what I can do to soothe their feelings."

And so, Hunter's daughter took the horn of water back to her husband who gave a loud snort when he took a drink. The snort turned into a bellow and all of the Buffalo got up in alarm. They all put their tails in the air and danced a Buffalo Dance over the hill, trampling the poor man to pieces who was still waiting for his daughter near the Buffalo wallow.

His daughter sat down on the edge of the wallow and broke into tears.

"Why are you crying?" said her Buffalo husband.

"You have killed my father and I am a prisoner, besides," she sobbed.

"Well, what of my people?" her husband replied. We have given our children, our parents and some of our wives up to your relatives in exchange for your presence among us. A deal is a deal."

But after some consideration of her feelings, Large Buffalo knelt down beside her and said to her, "If you can bring your father back to life again, we will let him take you back home to your people." So, Hunter's Daughter started to sing a little song. "Magpie, Magpie help me find some piece of my father which I can mend back whole again."

Magpie appeared and sat down in front of her with his head cocked to the side. "Magpie, Magpie, please see what you can find," she sang softly to the wind which bent the grasses slightly apart. Magpie cocked his head to the side and looked carefully within the layered folds of the grasses as the wind sighed again. Quickly he picked out a piece of her father that had been hidden there, a little bit of bone. "That will be enough to do the trick," said Hunter's Daughter, as she put the bone on the ground and covered it with her blanket.

And then she started to sing a reviving song that had the power to bring injured people back to the land of the living. Quietly she sang the song that her grandmother had taught her. After a few melodious passages, there was a lump under the blanket. She and Magpie looked under the blanket and could see a man, but the man was not breathing. He lay cold as stone. So, Hunter's Daughter continued to sing, a little softer, and a little softer, so as not to startle her father as he began to move. When he stood up, alive and strong, the Buffalo people were amazed. They said to Hunter's Daughter, "Will you sing this song for us after every hunt? We will teach your people the Buffalo Dance, so that whenever you dance before the hunt, you will be assured a good result. Then you will sing this song for us, and we will all come back to live again."

Origin of the Buffalo

Cheyenne

Long ago, a tribe of Cheyenne hunters lived at the head of a rushing stream, which eventually emptied into a large cave.

Because of the great need for a new food supply for his people, the Chief called a council meeting.

"We should explore the large cave," he told his people. "How many brave hunters will offer to go on this venture? Of course, it may be very dangerous, but we have brave hunters." No one responded to the Chief's request.

Finally, one young brave painted himself for hunting and stepped forth, replying to the Chief, "I will go and sacrifice myself for our people." He arrived at the cave, and to his surprise, First Brave found two other Cheyenne hunters near the opening, where the stream rushed underground.

"Are they here to taunt me," First Brave wondered? "Will they only pretend to jump when I do?"

But the other two braves assured him they would go.

"No, you are mistaken about us. We really do want to enter the cave with you," they said.

First Brave then joined hands with them and together they jumped into the huge opening of the cave. Because of the darkness, it took some time for their eyes to adjust. They then discovered what looked like a door. First Brave knocked, but there was no response. He knocked again, louder.

"What do you want, my brave ones?" asked an old Indian grandmother as she opened her door.

"Grandmother, we are searching for a new food supply for our tribe," First Brave replied. "Our people never seem to have enough food to eat."

"Are you hungry now?" she asked.

"Oh, yes, kind Grandmother, we are very hungry," all three braves answered.

The old grandmother opened her door wide, inviting the young braves to enter.

"Look out there!" she pointed for them to look through her window.

A beautiful wide prairie stretched before their eyes. Great herds of buffalo were grazing contentedly. The young hunters could hardly believe what they saw!

The old grandmother brought each of them a stone pan full of buffalo meat. How good it tasted, as they ate and ate until they were filled. To their surprise, more buffalo meat remained in their stone pans!

"I want you to take your stone pans of buffalo meat back to your people at your camp," said the old grandmother. "Tell them that soon I will send some live buffalo."

"Thank you, thank you, thank you, kind Grandmother," said the three young Cheyenne braves.

When the young hunters returned to their tribe with the gifts of buffalo meat, their people rejoiced over the new, good food. Their entire tribe ate heartily from the old grandmother's three magic pans, and were grateful.

When the Cheyennes waked at dawn the next day, herds of buffalo had mysteriously appeared, surrounding their village! They were truly thankful to the old Indian grandmother and to the Sky Spirits for their good fortune.

The Piqued Buffalo-Wife
Blackfoot
(Tales of the North American Indians by Stith Thompson 1929).

Once a young man went out and came to a buffalo-cow fast in the mire.

After a time, she gave birth to a boy. When he could run about, this boy would go into the Indian camps and join in the games of the children, but would always mysteriously disappear in the evening.

One day this boy told his mother that he intended to search among the camps for his father. Not long after this he was playing with the children in the camps as usual, and went into the lodge of a head man in company with a boy of the family. He told this head man that his father lived somewhere in the camp and that he was anxious to find him. The head man took pity on the boy, and sent out a messenger to call into his lodge all the old men in the camp.

When these were all assembled and standing around the lodge, the head man requested the boy to pick out his father. The boy looked them over and then told the head man that his father was not among them.

Then the head man sent out a messenger to call in all the men next in age but, when these were assembled, the boy said that his father was not among them. Again, the head man sent out the messenger to call in all the men of the next rank in age. When they were assembled, the boy looked them over as before, and announced that his father was not among them. So once again the head man sent out his messenger to call in all the young unmarried men of the camp.

As they were coming into the head man's lodge, the boy ran to one of them and, embracing him, said, "Here is my father."

After a time the boy told his father that he wished to take him to see his mother. The boy said, "When we come near her, she will run at you and hook four times, but you are to stand perfectly still."

The next day the boy and his father started out on their journey. As they were going along, they saw a buffalo-cow which immediately ran at them as the boy had predicted. The man stood perfectly still, and at the fourth time, as the cow was running forward to hook at him, she became a woman.

Then she went home with her husband and child.

One day shortly after their return, she warned her husband that whatever he might do he must never strike at her with fire.

They lived together happily for many years. She was a remarkably good woman.

One evening when the husband had invited some guests, and the woman expressed a dislike to prepare food for them, he became very angry and, catching up a stick from the fire, struck at her. As he did so, the woman and her child vanished, and the people saw a buffalo cow and calf running from the camp.

Now the husband was very sorry and mourned for his wife

and child. After a time, he went out to search for them. In order that he might approach the buffalo without being discovered, he rubbed himself with filth from a buffalo-wallow.

In the course of time he came to a place where some buffalo were dancing. He could hear them from a distance. As he was approaching, he met his son, who was now, as before, a buffalo-calf.

The father explained to the boy that he was mourning for him and his mother and that he had come to take them home. The calf-boy explained that this would be very difficult, for his father would be required to pass through an ordeal. The calf-boy explained to him that, when he arrived among the buffalo and inquired for his wife and son, the chief of the buffalo would order that he select his child from among all the buffalo-calves in the herd. Now the calf-boy wished to assist his father, and told him that he would know his child by a sign, because, when the calves appeared before him, his own child would hold up its tail.

Then the man proceeded until he came to the place where the buffalo were dancing. Immediately he was taken before the chief of the buffalo-herd. The chief required that he first prove his relationship to the child by picking him out from among all the other calves of the herd. The man agreed to this and the calves were brought up. He readily picked out his own child by the sign.

The chief of the buffalo, however, was not satisfied with this proof and said that the father could not have the child until he identified him four times. While the preparations were being made for another test, the calf-boy came to his father and explained that he would be known this time by closing one eye. When the time arrived, the calves were brought as before, and the chief of the buffalo directed the father to identify his child, which he did by the sign.

Before the next trial the calf-boy explained to his father that the sign would be one ear hanging down. Accordingly, when the calves were brought up for the father to choose, he again identified his child.

Now, before the last trial, the boy came again to his father and notified him that the sign by which he was to be known was dancing and holding up one leg. Now the calf-boy had a chum among the buffalo-calves, and when the calves were called up before the chief so that the father might select his child, the chum saw the calf-boy beginning to dance holding up one leg, and he thought to himself, "He is doing some fancy dancing." So, he, also, danced in the same way.

Now the father observed that there were two calves giving the sign, and realized that he must make a guess. He did so, but the guess was wrong. Immediately the herd rushed upon the man and trampled him into the dust. Then they all ran away except the calf-boy, his mother, and an old bull.

These three mourned together for the fate of the unfortunate man. After a time, the old bull requested that they examine the ground to see if they could find a piece of bone. After long and careful search, they succeeded in finding one small piece that had not been trampled by the buffalo. The bull took this piece, made a sweat-house, and finally restored the man to life.

When the man was restored, the bull explained to him that he and his family would receive some power, some head-dresses, some songs, and some crooked sticks, such as he had seen the buffalo carry in the dance at the time when he attempted to pick out his son.

The calf-boy and his mother then became human beings, and returned with the man. It was this man who started the Bull and the Horn Societies, and it was his wife who started the Matoki.

Splinter Foot Girl

An Arapaho Legend Dorsey and Kroeber, from "Anthropological Papers of the Field Museum", v 153, No. 81

It was in winter and a large party was on the war-path. Some of them became tired and went home, but seven continued on their way.

Coming to a river, they made camp on account of one of them who was weary and nearly exhausted.

They found that he was unable to go farther. Then they made a good brush hut in order that they might winter there. From this place they went out and looked for buffalo and hunted them wherever they thought they might find them.

During the hunting one of them ran against a thorny plant and became unable to hunt for some time. His leg swelled very much in consequence of the wound, and finally suddenly opened. Then a child came out from the leg. The young men took from their own clothes what they could spare and used it for wrapping for the child.

They made a panther skin answer as a cradle. They passed the child around from one to the other, like people smoking a pipe. They were glad to have another person with them and they were very fond of the child.

While they lived there, they killed very many elk and saved the teeth. From the skins they made a dress for the child, which was then old enough to run about. The dress was a girl's, entirely covered with elk teeth. They also made a belt for her. She was very beautiful. Her name was Foot Stuck Child.

A buffalo bull called Bone Bull heard that these young men had had a daughter born to them. As is the custom, he sent the magpie to go to these people to ask for the girl in marriage. The magpie came to the young men and told them what the Bone-bull wished; but he did not meet with any success.

The young men said, "We will not do it. We love our daughter. She is so young that it will not be well to let her go."

The magpie returned and told the Bone-bull what the young men had said. He advised the bull to get a certain small bird which was very clever and would perhaps persuade the young men to consent to the girl's marriage with him.

So, the small bird was sent out by the bull. It reached the place where the people lived and lighted on the top of the brush house. In a gentle voice it said to the men, "I am sent by Bone Bull to ask for your daughter."

The young men still refused, giving the same answer as before. The bird flew back and told the bull of the result. The bull said to it, "Go back and tell them that I mean what I ask. I shall come myself later." It was known that the bull was very powerful and hard to overcome or escape from. The bird went again and fulfilled the bull's instruction, but again returned unsuccessfully.

It told the bull: "They are at last making preparations for the marriage. They are dressing the girl finely." But the bull did not believe it.

Then, in order to free itself from the unpleasant task, the bird advised him to procure the services of someone who could do better than itself; some one that had a sweet juicy tongue. So, the bull sent another bird, called "Fire Owner," which has red on its head and reddish wings. This bird took the message to the young men. Now at last they consented.

So, the girl went to the bull and was received by him and lived with him for some time. She wore a painted buffalo robe. At certain times the bull got up in order to lead the herd to water. At such times he touched his wife, who, wearing her robe, was sitting in the same position as all the rest, as a sign for her to go too.

The young men were lonely and thought how they might recover their daughter. It was a year since she had left them. They sent out flies, but when the flies came near the bull, he bellowed to drive them away. The flies were so much afraid of him that they did not approach him. Then the magpie was sent, and came and alighted at a distance; but when the bull saw him, he said, "Go away! I do not want you about."

They sent the blackbird, which lit on his back and began to sing. But the bull said to it also: "Go away, I do not want you about."

The blackbird flew back to the men and said, " I can do nothing to help you to get your daughter back, but I will tell you of two animals that work unseen, and are very cunning: they are the mole and the badger. If you get their help, you will surely recover the girl."

Then the young men got the mole and the badger, and they started at night, taking arrows with them. They went underground, the mole going ahead. The badger followed and made the hole larger. They came under the place where the girl was sitting and the mole emerged under her blanket.

He gave her the arrows which he had brought and she stuck them into the ground and rested her robe on them and then the badger came under this too. The two animals said to her, "We have come to take you back." She said, " I am afraid," but they urged her to flee.

Finally, she consented, and leaving her robe in the position in which she always sat, went back through the hole with the mole and the badger to the house of the young men. When she arrived, they started to flee. The girl had become tired, when they came to the stone and asked it to help them. The stone said, "I can do nothing for you, the bull is too powerful to contend with."

They rested by the side of the stone; then they continued on their way, one of them carrying the girl. But they went more slowly on account of her. They crossed a river, went through the timber, and on the prairie the girl walked again for a distance. In front of them they saw a lone immense cottonwood tree.

They said to it: "We are pursued by a powerful animal and come to you for help."

The tree told them, "Run around me four times," and they did this. The tree had seven large branches, the lowest of them high enough to be out of the reach of the buffalo, and at the top was a fork in which was a nest. They climbed the tree, each of the men sitting on one of the branches, and the girl getting into the nest. So, they waited for the bull who would pursue them.

When the bull touched his wife in order to go to water, she did not move. He spoke to her angrily and touched her again. The third time he tried to hook her with his horn, but tossed the empty robe away. "They cannot escape me," he said.

He noticed the fresh ground which the badger had thrown up in order to close the hole. He hooked the ground and threw it to one side, and the other bulls got up and did the same, throwing the ground as if they were making a ditch and following the course of the underground passage until they came to the place where the people had lived. The camp was already broken up, but they followed the people's trail.

Coming to the stone, the bull asked, "Have you hidden the people or done anything to help them?"

The stone said: "I have not helped them for fear of you."

But the bull insisted: "Tell me where you hid them. I know that they reached you and are somewhere about."

"No, I did not hide them; they reached this place but went on," said the stone.

"Yes, you have hidden them; I can smell them and see their tracks about here."

"The girl rested here a short time; that is what you smell," said the stone.

Then the buffalo followed the trail again and crossed the river, the bull leading. One calf which was becoming very tired tried hard to keep up with the rest. It became exhausted at the lone cottonwood tree and stopped to rest. But the herd went on, not having seen the people in the tree. They went far on.

The girl was so tired that she had a slight hemorrhage. Then she sat down.

As the calf was resting in the shade below, the bloody spittle fell down before it. The calf smelled it, knew it, got up, and went after the rest of the buffalo. Coming near the herd, it cried out to the bull: "Stop! I have found a girl in the top of a tree. She is the one who is your wife."

Then the whole herd turned back to the tree.

When they reached it, the bull said: "We will surely get you."

The tree said: "You have four parts of strength. I give you a chance to do something to me."

Then the buffalo began to attack the tree; those with least strength began. They butted it until its thick bark was peeled off. Meanwhile the young men were shooting them from the tree.

The tree said: "Let some of them break their horns."

Then came the large bulls, who split the wood of the tree; but some stuck fast, and others broke their horns or lost the covering.

The bull said, "I will be the last one and will make the tree fall." At last, he came on, charging against the tree from the southeast, striking it, and making a big gash. Then, coming from the southwest, he made a larger hole. Going to the northwest, he charged from there, and again cut deeper, but broke his right horn. Going then to the northeast, he charged the tree with his left horn and made a still larger hole. The fifth time he went straight east, intending to strike the tree in the center and break it down.

He pranced about, raising the dust; but the tree said to him: "You can do nothing. So come on quickly." This made him angry and he charged. The tree said: "This time you will stick fast," and he ran his left horn far into the middle of the wood and stuck fast. Then the tree told the young men to shoot him in the soft part of his neck and sides, for he could not get loose or injure them.

Then they shot him and killed him, so that he hung there. Then they cut him loose.

The tree told them to gather all the chips and pieces of wood that had been knocked off and cover the bull with them, and they did so. All the buffalo that had not been killed went away. The tree said to them: "Hereafter you will be overcome by human beings. You will have horns, but when they come to hunt you, you will be afraid. You will be killed and eaten by them and they will use your skins.

Then the buffalo scattered over the land with half-broken, short horns.

After the people had descended from the tree, they went on their way. The magpie came to them as messenger sent by Merciless-man to ask the young men for their daughter in marriage. He was a round rock. The magpie knew what this rock had done and warned the men not to consent to the marriage.

He said, "Do not have anything to do with him, since he is not a good man. Your daughter is beautiful, and I do not like to see her married to the rock. He has married the prettiest girls he could hear of, obtaining them somehow. But his wives are crippled, one-armed, or one-legged, or much bruised. I will tell the rock to get the hummingbird for a messenger because that bird is swift and can escape him if he should pursue."

So, the magpie returned and said that the young men refused the marriage. But the rock sent him back to say: "Tell them that the girl must marry me nevertheless." The magpie persuaded him to send the hummingbird as messenger instead of himself.

Then the hummingbird went to carry the message to the young men; but, on reaching them, told them instead: "He is merciless and not the right man to marry this girl. He has treated his wives very badly. You had better leave this place."

So, he went back without having tried to help the rock. He told the rock that he had seen neither camp nor people.

"Yes, you saw them," said the rock; "you are trying to help them instead of helping me. Therefore, you try to pretend that you did not see them. Go back and tell them that I want the girl. If they refuse, say that I shall be there soon."

The hummingbird went again to the men and told them what the rock wished, and said: "He is powerful. Perhaps it is best if you let your daughter go. But there are two animals that can surely help you. They can bring her back before he injures her. They are the mole and the badger."

"Yes," they said, now having confidence in these animals.

So, the hummingbird took the girl to the rock. He reached his tent, which was large and fine, but full of crippled wives. "I have your wife here," he said.

"Very well," said the rock, "let her come in. I am pleased that you brought her; she is pretty enough for me."

Soon after the hummingbird had left with the girl, the mole and the badger started underground and made their way to the rock's tent. In the morning the rock always went buzzing out through the top of the tent; in the evening he came back home in the same way. While he was away, the two animals arrived. The girl was sitting with both feet outstretched.

They said to her, "Remain sitting thus until your husband returns." Then they made a hole large enough for the rock to fall into and covered it lightly. In the evening the rock was heard coming. As he was entering above, the girl got up, and the rock dropped into the hole while she ran out of the tent saying: "Let the hole be closed."

"Let the earth be covered again," said the mole and the badger. They heard the rock inside the earth, tossing about, buzzing, and angry. The girl returned to her fathers.

They traveled all night, fleeing. In the morning the rock overtook them. As they were going, they wished a canyon with steep cliffs to be behind them. The rock went down the precipice, and while he tried to climb up again, the others went on. It became night again and in the morning the rock was near them once more.

Then the girl said: "This time it shall happen. I am tired and weary from running, my fathers." She was carrying a ball, and, saying: "First for my father," she threw it up and as it came down kicked it upwards, and her father rose up. Then she did the same for the others until all had gone up. When she came to do it for herself the rock was near. She threw the ball, kicked it, and she too rose up.

She said, "We have passed through dangers on my account; I think this is the best place for us to go. It is a good place where we are. I shall provide the means of living for you." To the rock she said. "You shall remain where you overtook us. You shall not trouble people any longer, but be found wherever there are hills."

She and her fathers reached the sky in one place. They live in a tent covered with stars.

The Quill-Work Girl and Her Seven Brothers

A Cheyenne Legend

Hundreds of years ago there was a girl who was very good at quill work, so good that she was the best among all the tribes everywhere. Her designs were radiant with color, and she could decorate anything -- clothing, pouches, quivers, even tipi's.

One day this girl sat down in her parents' lodge and began to make a man's outfit of white buckskin -- war shirt, leggings, moccasins, gauntlets, everything. It took her weeks to embroider them with exquisite quill work and fringes of buffalo hair marvelous to look at. Though her mother said nothing, she wondered. The girl had no brothers, nor was a young man courting her, so why was she making a man's outfit?

As if life wasn't strange enough, no sooner had she finished the first outfit than she began working on a second, then on a third. She worked all year until she had made and decorated seven complete sets of men's clothes, the last a very small one. The mother just watched and kept wondering. At last, after the girl had finished the seventh outfit, she spoke to her mother. "Someplace, many days' walk from here, lives seven brothers," she said. "Someday all the world will admire them. Since I am an only child, I want to take them for my brothers, and these clothes are for them."

"It is well, my daughter," her mother said. "I will go with you."

"This is too far for you to walk," said the girl.

"Then I will go part of the way," said her mother.

They loaded their strongest dogs with the seven bundles and set off toward the north. "You seem to know the way," said the mother.

"Yes, I don't know why, but I do," answered the daughter.

"And you seem to know all about these seven young men and what makes them stand out from ordinary humans."

"I know about them," said the girl, "though I don't know how."

Thus, they walked, the girl seeming sure of herself. At last, the mother said, "This is as far as I can go." They divided the dogs, the girl keeping two for her journey, and took leave of each other. Then the mother headed south back to her village and her husband, while her daughter continued walking into the north.

At last, the daughter came to a lone, painted, and very large tipi which stood near a wide stream. The stream was shallow and she waded across it, calling: "It is I, the young-girl-looking-for-brothers, bringing gifts."

At that a small boy about ten years old came out of the tipi. "I am the youngest of seven brothers," he told the girl. "The others are out hunting buffalo, but they'll come back after a while. I have been expecting you. But you'll be a surprise to my brothers, because they don't have my special gifts of `No Touch'."

"What is the gift of no touch?" asked the girl.

"Sometime you'll find out. Well, come into the tipi."

The girl gave the boy the smallest outfit, which fitted him perfectly and delighted him with its beautiful quill work.

"I shall take you all for my brothers," the girl told him.

"And I am glad to have you for a sister," answered the boy.

The girl took all the other bundles off her two dogs' backs and told them to go back to her parents, and at once the dogs began trotting south.

Inside the tipi were seven beds of willow sticks and sage. The girl unpacked her bundles and put a war shirt, a pair of leggings, a pair of moccasins, and a pair of gauntlets upon each of the older brothers' beds. Then she gathered wood and built a fire. From her packs she took dried meat, choke cherries, and kidney fat, and cooked a meal for eight.

Toward evening just as the meal was ready, the six older brothers appeared laden with buffalo meat. The little boy ran outside the lodge and capered, kicking his heels and jumping up and down, showing off his quilled buckskin outfit.

"Where did you get these fine clothes?" the brothers asked.

"We have a new sister," said the child. "She's waiting inside, and she has clothes for you too. She does the most wonderful quill work in the world. And she's beautiful herself!"

The brothers greeted the girl joyfully. They were struck with wonder at the white buckskin outfits she had brought as gifts for them. They were as glad to have a sister to care for as she was to have brothers to cook and make clothes for. Thus, they lived happily.

One day after the older brothers had gone out to hunt, a light-colored buffalo- calf appeared at the tipi and scratched and knocked with his hoof against the entrance flap. The boy came out and asked it what it wanted.

"I am sent by the buffalo nation," said the calf. "We have heard of your beautiful sister, and we want her for our own."

"You can't have her," answered the boy. "Go away."

"Oh well, then somebody bigger than I will come," said the calf and ran off jumping and kicking its heels.

The next day when the boy and the sister were alone again, a young heifer arrived, lowing and snorting, rattling the entrance flap of the tipi.

Once more the child came out to ask what she wanted.

"I am sent by the buffalo nation," said the heifer. "We want your beautiful sister for ourselves."

"You can't have her," said the boy. "Go away!"

"Then somebody bigger than I will come," said the heifer, galloping off like the calf before her.

On the third day a large buffalo cow, grunting loudly, appeared at the lodge. The boy came out and asked, "Big buffalo cow, what do you want?"

"I am sent by the buffalo nation," said the cow. "I have come to take your beautiful sister. We want her."

"You can't have her," said the boy. "Go away!"

"Somebody very big will come after me," said the buffalo cow, "and he won't come alone. He'll kill you if you don't give him your sister." With these words the cow trotted off.

On the fourth day the older brothers stayed home to protect the girl. The earth began to tremble a little, then to rock and heave. At last appeared the most gigantic buffalo bull in the world, much larger than any you see now. Behind him came the whole buffalo nation, making the earth shudder. Pawing the ground, the huge bull snorted and bellowed like thunder. The six older brothers, peering out through the entrance hole, were very much afraid, but the little boy stepped boldly outside. "Big, oversized buffalo bull, what do you want from us?" he asked.

"I want your sister," said the giant buffalo bull. "If you won't give her to me, I'll kill you all."

The boy called for his sister and older brothers to come out. Terrified, they did so.

"I'll take her now," growled the huge bull.

"No," said the boy, "she doesn't want to be taken. You can't have her. Go away!"

"In that case I'll kill you now," roared the giant bull. "I'm coming!"

"Quick, brother, use your special medicine!" the six older brothers cried to the youngest.

"I am using it," said he. "Now all of you, catch hold of the branches of this tree. Hurry!" He pointed to a tree growing by the tipi. The girl and the six brothers jumped up into its branches. The boy took his bow and swiftly shot an arrow into the tree's trunk, then clasped the trunk tightly himself. At once the tree started to grow, shooting up into the sky in no time at all. It all happened much, much quicker than it can be told.

The brothers and the girl were lifted up in the tree branches, out of reach of the buffalo. They watched the herd of angry animals grunting and snorting, milling around the tree far below.

"I'll chop the tree down with my horns!" roared the giant buffalo. He charged the tree, which shook like a willow and swayed back and forth. Trying not to fall off, the girl and the brothers clutched the branches. The big bull had gouged a large piece of wood from the trunk.

The little boy said, "I'd better use one more arrow." He shot another arrow high into the treetop, and again the tree grew, shooting up another thousand feet or so, while the seven brothers and the girl rose with it.

The giant buffalo bull made his second charge. Again, his horns stabbed into the tree and splintered wood far and wide. The gash in the trunk had become larger.

The boy said, "I must shoot another arrow." He did, hitting the treetop again, and quick as a flash the tree rose another thousand feet.

A third time the bull charged, rocking the tree, making it sway from side to side so that the brothers and the girl almost tumbled out of their branches. They cried to the boy to save them. The child shot a fourth arrow into the tree, which rose again so that the seven young men and the girl disappeared into the clouds. The gash in the tree trunk had become dangerously large.

"When that bull charges again, he will shatter this tree," said the girl. "Little brother, help us!"

Just as the bull charged for the fourth time, the child let loose a single arrow he had left, and the tree rose above the clouds.

"Quick, step out right on the clouds. Hurry!" cried the little boy. "Don't be afraid!"

The bull's head hit the tree trunk with a fearful impact. His horns cut the trunk in two, but just as the tree slowly began to topple, the seven brothers and the girl stepped off its branches and into the sky.

There the eight of them stood. "Little brother, what will become of us now? We can never return to earth; we're up too high. What shall we do?"

"Don't grieve," said the little boy, "I'll turn us into stars."

At once the seven brothers and the girl were bathed in radiant light. They formed themselves into what the white men call the Big Dipper. You can see them there now. The brightest star is the beautiful girl, who is filling the sky with glimmering quill work, and the star twinkling at the very end of the Dipper's handle is the little boy. Can you see him?

Buffalo Hunting of The Plains

Cochiti
(Tales of the Cochiti Indians by Ruth Benedict
Bureau of American Ethnology Bulletin No. 98
1932)

We went from here in August. We had horses with three poles fastened to them for a travois, and we had one wagon drawn by oxen. We went a day's journey and slept in a canyon. Next day we came to Pecos. In the morning we went on again and came to San José. The next night we camped at Turkey River. After that we traveled day and night. We came out on the Plains at a great body of water that was called Green Lake. From there we went north all the time. We camped at a rocky place called the Cross. A day's journey north from there we came to a camp of Mexicans. I said to Antonio (his chum), "Here is lots of meat." These Mexicans were good hunters and they gave us food.

In the morning our leader told us, "Be ready to hunt." He took his long buffalo stick 9 and tied a piece of his fringed leggings to the top of it. I said to Antonio, "Let us go after the hunter and see him kill the buffalo." He went out. We saw a solitary buffalo coming to a pond to drink. He waded in, and when he was fast in the mud, the leader went up close on horseback and noosed him. He drew the rope tight and pulled him out of the pond. He spread out the carcass and took the skin and some of the meat, but he left the greater part because it would spoil. He went back to camp.

Next day we rested. That night we went to the Mexican camp and told them to get their people together; we would form a party together to go out hunting on the plains. The Mexicans received us well, and said, "To-morrow we will go." He (Mexican leader) guided us a whole day's trip. At midnight we came to the camping place. There was a lot of water there and we were all thirsty. He said, "Go and drink." We went down to the water but the brush grew so thick we could not reach it.

Next day we went on. The Indians and the Mexicans separated, the Mexicans going one way and the Indians another. At a place called Kapolina we came upon the buffalo. Two of the men had bows and arrows, the leader had a spear, and I had a gun. We were all on horseback and we killed six buffalo. We cut them and skinned them and packed the meat and skins on the four horses. It was late when we got to the place where we had camped. There were lots of people there and we hid, for we were frightened. Then we saw that they were hunters from Santo

Domingo and from Santa Clara and from Sandia, who had arrived that day. We all stayed four days there. The Indians of the other pueblos asked our leader if he would lead their hunting party; we held a council with them and planned to go hunting together.

That night we cut the six buffalo in strips and spread the meat on the grass to dry it. The fat we hung from the cedar bushes. We made a feast for all the three pueblos, and put slabs of meat on the coals and cracked the bones for the marrow.

After four days we went out all together on a hunt. It was a big hunt for all the other pueblos were with us. We went north. As we were passing an arroyo I saw a buffalo coming and I went after him. I killed it in the arroyo. A Santo Domingo Indian came up and said, "Shall I help you cut it up?" "No, this buffalo is only three years old. I can manage it by myself." We all came back to camp bringing the buffalo we had killed. That night we sliced the meat and hung the fat to dry. Each man was given the same amount and the one who worked fastest went to bed first. We stayed there a week. Every night the people of the other pueblos came to the Cochiti camp and danced, and were paid with meat. We had great piles of dried buffalo meat all ready to carry home. All our provisions were gone, and we ate nothing but buffalo meat. The buffalo fat we used just like bread. It snowed and we went hunting again. It was very cold. Two Santa Clara hunters and two Sandia hunters were nearly frozen. They could not go any farther through the snow. We went out to look for them, and found them sitting in the snow with their legs frozen. We took them to camp. They hobbled on sticks.

Next night we were ready to come home. We sent messengers ahead to the home pueblos to tell them we were starting back. Antonio told me how to lead the horses, how to pile dry meat on the buffalo skin and place the load on the horses and tie it up. Next day we started, and that night we came to the place where we had killed the buffalo that was stuck in the mud. We rested that day. Then we started again. That day we traveled on soft dirt, but the next day we had a hard road. We traveled night and day for three days and three nights. Finally, we came to Tucumcare. We stayed all day and rested. The next day we got to Red Paint place, and we gathered paint to bring home (as always, when they made this trip). We got to Pajarito that night. We danced all night and told stories. The next day we got to Turkey River (Mexican settlement). We stayed there all day. We had the tongue of the wagon repaired and paid for it with meat. We traded two or three oxen that were exhausted, for fresh oxen.

The next day the messenger from Cochiti returned. He said that our message had come to Cochiti and that they were getting ready for us there. He brought food to each of the Cochiti hunters from our wives. I had a little baby. My wife had taken the hand of our baby and marked the dough with it, and the bread in my lunch was marked with our baby's hand. The messenger told me, "Hurry, your father and mother are very homesick for you." I could not wait to get home. I started on alone, and that night I slept alone at San José River. I went on to Baca Ojo. People had told me, "Be careful, my friend, there are lots of thieves there." I traveled all day alone, and got to Baca Ojo. They begged me to stay there, and asked me to put my mule in the barn.

I came on the next day to Galisteo, and from there I came in one day to Cochiti. In the morning I came to a Mexican settlement. They said, "Buffalo hunter, give me some grease, give me some meat." They took me to their houses. I said, "I will give you some, I am not as hungry as you

Mexicans are." They took me into their houses and gave me good things to eat and let me, rest a little. They were hungry for the buffalo meat. I came to La Bajara Canyon. At home they were watching for me, and went to my mother and father and told them that their son was coming. My people were excited, and they went down to the river to meet me. My father was very old, and my mother and father cried when they saw me. I said to them, "Why are you thinking so much about me? I am well. I've grown fat." We all went together to my house.

How the Buffalo Hunt Began

Cheyenne Legend

The buffalo formerly ate man. The magpie and the hawk were on the side of the people, for neither ate the other or the people. These two birds flew away from a council between animals and men. They determined that a race would be held, the winners to eat the losers.

The course was long, around a mountain. The swiftest buffalo was a cow called Neika, "swift head." She believed she would win and entered the race. On the other hand, the people were afraid because of the long distance. They were trying to get medicine to prevent fatigue.

All the birds and animals painted themselves for the race, and since that time they have all been brightly colored. Even the water turtle put red paint around his eyes. The magpie painted himself white on head, shoulders, and tail. At last, all were ready for the race, and stood in a row for the start.

They ran and ran, making some loud noises in place of singing to help themselves to run faster. All small birds, turtles, rabbits, coyotes, wolves, flies, ants, insects, and snakes were soon left far behind. When they approached the mountain, the buffalo-cow was ahead. Then came the magpie, hawk, and the people. The rest were strung out along the way. Dust rose so that nothing could be seen.

All around the mountain the buffalo-cow led the race, but the two birds knew they could win, and merely kept up with her until they neared the finish line, which was back at the starting place. Then both birds swept by her and won the race for man. As they flew the course, they had seen fallen animals and birds all over the place who had run themselves to death turning the ground and rocks red from their blood.

The buffalo then told their young to hide from the people, who were going out to hunt them and also told them to take some human flesh with them for the last time. The young buffaloes did this and stuck that meat in front of their chests beneath the throat. Therefore, the people do not eat that part of the buffalo, saying it is part human flesh.

From that day forward the Cheyennes began to hunt buffalo. Since all the friendly animals and birds were on the people's side, they are not eaten by people, but they do wear and use their beautiful feathers for ornaments.

Another version adds that when coyote, who was on the side of buffalo, finished the race, the magpie who even beat the hawk, said to coyote, "We will not eat you, but only use your skin."

Origin of the Animals

Jicarilla-Apache

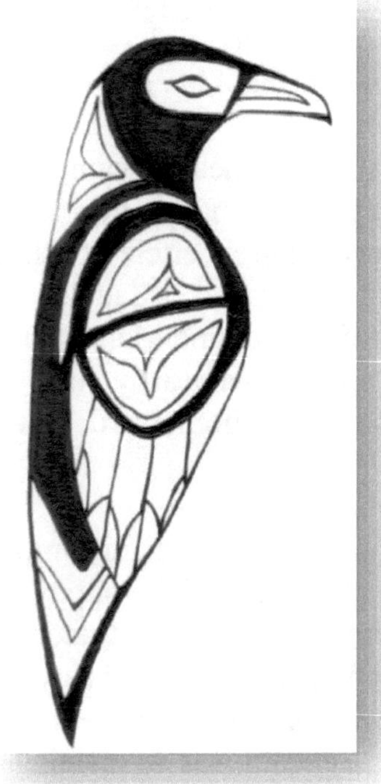

When Apaches emerged from the underworld, they travelled southward for four days. They had no other food than two kinds of seeds, which they ground between two stones.

Near where they camped on the fourth night, one tepee stood apart from the others. While the owner and his wife were absent for a short time, a Raven brought a quiver of arrows and a bow, hanging them on the lodge pole. When the children came out of the lodge, they took down the quiver and found some meat inside. They ate it and instantly became very fat.

Upon her return, the mother noticed grease on the hands and faces of her children, who told her what had happened. The woman hurried to tell her husband the tale. All the tribe marveled at the wonderful food that made the children so fat. How they hoped the Raven might soon return with more of his good food.

When Raven discovered that his meat had been stolen, he flew eastward to his mountain home beyond the normal range of man. A bat followed Raven and later informed the Apaches where Raven lived. That night the Apache Chief called a council meeting. They decided to send a delegation to try and obtain some of Raven's special kind of meat.

In four days, the Apache delegation reached the camp of the ravens, but could not obtain the information they desired. They discovered, however, a great circle of ashes where the ravens ate their meals. The Apaches decided to spy upon the ravens. That night the Medicine Man changed an Apache boy into a puppy to spy from a nearby bush. The main delegation broke camp and started homeward, leaving behind the puppy.

Next morning the ravens examined the abandoned camp of the Apaches. One of the young ravens found the puppy and was so pleased, he asked for permission to keep it under his blanket. Toward sunset, the puppy peaked out and saw an old raven brush aside some ashes from the fireplace. He then removed a large flat stone. Beneath was an opening through which the old raven disappeared. But when he returned, he led a buffalo, which was then killed and eaten by all the ravens.

For four days the puppy spied upon the ravens, and each evening a buffalo was brought up from the depths and devoured. Now that he was certain where the ravens obtained their good food, the puppy resumed his normal shape.

Early on the fifth morning, with a white feather in one hand and a black one in the other, he descended through the opening beneath the fireplace.

In the underworld, he saw four buffaloes and placed the white feather in the mouth of the nearest one. He commanded it to follow him. But the first buffalo told him to take the feather to the last buffalo. This he did, but the fourth buffalo sent him again to the first one, into whose mouth the boy thrust the white feather.

"You are now the King of the Animals," declared the boy.

Upon returning to the above-world, the boy was followed by all the animals present upon the earth at that time. As the large herd passed through the opening, one of the ravens awoke, hurrying to close the lid. Upon seeing that all the animals willingly followed the Apache boy, the raven exclaimed, "When you kill any of the animals, remember to save the eyes for me."

For four days the boy followed the tracks of the Apaches and overtook them with his giant herd of animals. Soon they all returned to the camp of the Apaches, where the Chief slew the first buffalo for a feast that followed. The boy remembered and saved the eyes for the ravens.

One old grandmother who lived in a brush lodge was annoyed with one of the deer that ate some of her lodge covering. Snatching a stick from the fire, she struck the deer's nose and the white ash stuck there leaving a white mark that can still be seen on the descendants of that deer.

"Hereafter, you shall avoid mankind," she pronounced. "Your nose will tell you when you are too close to them."

Thus ended the short period of harmony between man and the animals. Each day the animals wandered farther and farther from the tribes. Apaches prayed that the animals would return so they could enjoy the good meat again. It is mostly at night when the deer appear, but not too close, because the old grandmother told them to be guided by their noses!

Apaches developed skill in using the bows and arrows to hunt the good animal meat they liked so much, especially the buffalo.

The Buffalo Rock

Blackfoot Lodge Tales, George Bird Grinnell, [1892]

A small stone, which is usually a fossil shell of some kind, is known by the Blackfeet as I-nis´-kim, the buffalo stone. This object is strong medicine, and, as indicated in some of these stories, gives its possessor great power with buffalo. The stone is found on the prairie, and the person who succeeds in obtaining one is regarded as very fortunate. Sometimes a man, who is riding along on the prairie, will hear a peculiar faint chirp, such as a little bird might utter. The sound he knows is made by a buffalo rock. He stops and searches on the ground for the rock, and if he cannot find it, marks the place and very likely returns next day, either alone or with others from the camp, to look for it again. If it is found, there is great rejoicing. How the first buffalo rock was obtained, and its power made known, is told in the following story.

Long ago, in the winter time, the buffalo suddenly disappeared. The snow was so deep that the people could not move in search of them, for in those days they had no horses. So, the hunters killed deer, elk, and other small game along the river bottoms, and when these were all killed off or driven away, the people began to starve.

One day, a young married man killed a jack-rabbit. He was so hungry that he ran home as fast as he could, and told one of his wives to hurry and get some water to cook it. While the young woman was going along the path to the river, she heard a beautiful song. It sounded close by, but she looked all around and could see no one.

The song seemed to come from a cotton-wood tree near the path. Looking closely at this tree she saw a queer rock jammed in a fork, where the tree was split, and with it a few hairs from a buffalo, which had rubbed there. The woman was frightened and dared not pass the tree. Pretty soon the singing stopped, and the I-nis´-kim [buffalo rock] spoke to the woman and said: "Take me to your lodge, and when it is dark, call in the people and teach them the song you have just heard. Pray, too, that you may not starve, and that the buffalo may come back. Do this, and when day comes, your hearts will be glad."

The woman went on and got some water, and when she came back, took the rock and gave it to her husband, telling him about the song and what the rock had said. As soon as it was dark, the man called the chiefs and old men to his lodge, and his wife taught them this song. They prayed, too, as the rock had said should be done. Before long, they heard a noise far off. It was the tramp of a great herd of buffalo coming. Then they knew that the rock was very powerful, and, ever since that, the people have taken care of it and prayed to it.

[NOTE. —I-nis´-kims are usually small *Ammonites*, or sections of *Baculites,* or sometimes merely oddly shaped nodules of flint. It is said of them that if an I-nis´-kim is wrapped up and left undisturbed for a long time, it will have young ones; two small stones similar in shape to the original one will be found in the package with it.]

The Origins of the Buffalo Dance

When the buffalo first came to be upon the land, they were not friendly to the people. When the hunters tried to coax them over the cliffs for the good of the villages, they were reluctant to offer themselves up. They did not relish being turned into blankets and dried flesh for winter rations. They did not want their hooves and horn to become tools and utensils nor did they welcome their sinew being used for sewing. "No, no," they said. We won't fall into your traps. And we will not fall for your tricks." So, when the hunters guided them towards the abyss, they would always turn aside at the very last moment. With this lack of cooperation, it seemed the villagers would be hungry and cold and ragged all winter long.

Now one of the hunters had a daughter who was very proud of her father's skill with the bow. During the fullness of summer, he always brought her the best of hides to dress, and she in turn would work the deerskins into the softest, whitest of garments for him to wear. Her own dresses were like the down of a snow goose, and the moccasins she made for the children and the grandmothers in the village were the most welcome of gifts.

But now with the hint of snow on the wind, and deer becoming more scarce in the willow breaks, she could see this reluctance on the part of the buffalo families could become a real problem.

Hunter's Daughter decided she would do something about it.

She went to the base of the cliff and looked up. She began to sing in a low, soft voice, "Oh, buffalo family, come down and visit me. If you come down and feed my relatives in a wedding feast, I will join your family as the bride of your strongest warrior."

She stopped and listened. She thought she heard the slight rumbling sound of thunder in the distance.

Again, she sang, "Oh, buffalo family, come down and visit me. Feed my family in a wedding feast so that I may be a bride."

The thunder was much louder now. Suddenly the buffalo family began falling from the sky at her feet.

One very large bull landed on top of the others, and walked across the backs of his relatives to stand before Hunter's Daughter.

"I am here to claim you as my bride," said Large Buffalo.

"Oh, but now I am afraid to go with you," said Hunter's Daughter.

"Ah, but you must," said Large Buffalo, "For my people have come to provide your people with a wedding feast. As you can see, they have offered themselves up."

"Yes, but I must run and tell my relatives the good news," said Hunter's Daughter. "No," said Large Buffalo. No word need be sent. You are not getting away so easily."

And with that said, Large Buffalo lifted her between his horns and carried her off to his village in the rolling grass hills.

The next morning the whole village was out looking for Hunter's Daughter. When they found the mound of buffalo below the cliff, the father, who was in fact a fine tracker as well as a skilled hunter, looked at his daughter's footprints in the dust.

"She's gone off with a buffalo, he said. I shall follow them and bring her back."

So, Hunter walked out upon the plains, with only his bow and arrows as companions. He walked and walked a great distance until he was so tired that he had to sit down to rest beside a buffalo wallow.

Along came Magpie and sat down beside him.

Hunter spoke to Magpie in a respectful tone, "O knowledgeable bird, has my daughter been stolen from me by a buffalo? Have you seen them? Can you tell me where they have gone?"

Magpie replied with understanding, "Yes, I have seen them pass this way. They are resting just over this hill."

"Well," said Hunter, would you kindly take my daughter a message for me? Will you tell her I am here just over the hill?"

So, Magpie flew to where Large Buffalo lay asleep amidst his relatives in the dry prairie grass. He hopped over to where Hunter's Daughter was quilling moccasins, as she sat dutifully beside her sleeping husband. "Your father is waiting for you on the other side of the hill," whispered Magpie to the maiden.

"Oh, this is very dangerous," she told him. These buffalo are not friendly to us and they might try to hurt my father if he should come this way. Please tell him to wait for me and I will try to slip away to see him."

Just then her husband, Large Buffalo, awoke and took off his horn. "Go bring me a drink from the wallow just over this hill," said her husband.

So, she took the horn in her hand and walked very casually over the hill.

Her father motioned silently for her to come with him, as he bent into a low crouch in the grass. "No," she whispered. The buffalo are angry with our people who have killed their people. They will run after us and trample us into the dirt. I will go back and see what I can do to soothe their feelings."

And so, Hunter's daughter took the horn of water back to her husband who gave a loud snort when he took a drink. The snort turned into a bellow and all of the buffalo got up in alarm. They all put their tails in the air and danced a buffalo dance over the hill, trampling the poor man to pieces who was still waiting for his daughter near the buffalo wallow.

His daughter sat down on the edge of the wallow and broke into tears.

"Why are you crying?" said her buffalo husband.

"You have killed my father and I am a prisoner, besides," she sobbed.

"Well, what of my people?" her husband replied. We have given our children, our parents and some of our wives up to your relatives in exchange for your presence among us. A deal is a deal."

But after some consideration of her feelings, Large Buffalo knelt down beside her and said to her, "If you can bring your father back to life again, we will let him take you back home to your people."

So, Hunter's Daughter started to sing a little song. "Magpie, Magpie help me find some piece of my father which I can mend back whole again."

Magpie appeared and sat down in front of her with his head cocked to the side.

"Magpie, Magpie, please see what you can find," she sang softly to the wind which bent the grasses slightly apart. Magpie cocked his head to the side and looked carefully within the layered folds of the grasses as the wind sighed again. Quickly he picked out a piece of her father that had been hidden there, a little bit of bone.

"That will be enough to do the trick," said Hunter's Daughter, as she put the bone on the ground and covered it with her blanket.

And then she started to sing a reviving song that had the power to bring injured people back to the land of the living. Quietly she sang the song that her grandmother had taught her. After a few melodious passages, there was a lump under the blanket. She and Magpie looked under the blanket and could see a man, but the man was not breathing. He lay cold as stone. So, Hunter's Daughter continued to sing, a little softer, and a little softer, so as not to startle her father as he began to move. When he stood up, alive and strong, the buffalo people were amazed. They said to Hunter's Daughter, "Will you sing this song for us after every hunt? We will teach your people the buffalo dance, so that whenever you dance before the hunt, you will be assured a good result. Then you will sing this song for us, and we will all come back to live again."

White Buffalo Woman

This is a central myth of the Plains tribes, especially the Lakota, or Sioux. It tells how the Lakota first received their sacred pipe and the ceremony in which to use it. It has often been related, for example by Black Elk, Lame Deer and Looks for Buffalo.

In the days before the Lakota had horses on which to hunt the buffalo, food was often scarce. One summer when the Lakota nation had camped together, there was very little to eat. Two young men of the Itazipcho band – the 'Without-Bows' – decided they would rise early and look for game. They left the camp while the dogs were still yawning, and set out across the plain, accompanied only by the song of the yellow meadowlark.

After a while the day began to grow warm. Crickets chirruped in the waving grass, prairie dogs darted into their holes as the braves approached, but still there was no real game. So, the young men made towards a little hill from which they would see further across the vast expanse of level prairie. Reaching it, they shielded their eyes and scanned the distance, but what they saw coming out of the growing heat haze was something bright, that seemed to go on two legs, not four. In a while they could see that it was a very beautiful woman in shining white buckskin.

As the woman came closer, they could see that her buckskin was wonderfully decorated with sacred designs in rainbow-colored porcupine quills. She carried a bundle on her back, and a fan of fragrant sage leaves in her hand. Her jet-black hair was loose, except for a single strand tied with buffalo fur. Her eyes were full of light and power, and the young men were transfixed.

Now one of the men was filled with a burning desire. 'What a woman!' he said sideways to his friend. 'And all alone on the prairie. I'm going to make the most of this!'

'You fool,' said the other. 'This woman is holy.'

But the foolish one had made up his mind, and when the woman beckoned him towards her, he needed no second invitation. As he reached out for her, they were both enveloped in a great cloud. When it lifted, the woman stood there, while at her feet was nothing but a pile of bones with terrible snakes writhing among them.

'Behold,' said the woman to the good brave. 'I am coming to your people with a message from Tatanka Oyate, the buffalo nation. Return to Chief Standing Hollow Horn and tell him what you have seen. Tell him to prepare a tipi large enough for all his people, and to get ready for my coming.'

The young man ran back across the prairie and was gasping for breath as he reached his camp. With a small crowd of people already following him, he found Standing Hollow Horn and told him what had happened, and that the woman was coming. The chief ordered several tipis to be combined into one big enough for his band. The people waited excitedly for the woman to arrive.

After four days the scouts posted to watch for the holy woman saw something coming towards them in a beautiful manner from across the prairie. Then suddenly the woman was in the great lodge, walking round it in a sunwise direction. She stopped before Standing Hollow Horn in the west of the lodge, and held her bundle before him in both hands.

'Look on this,' she said, 'and always love and respect it. No one who is impure should ever touch this bundle, for it contains the sacred pipe.'

She unrolled the skin bundle and took out a pipe, and a small round stone which she put down on the ground.

'With this pipe you will walk on the earth, which is your grandmother and your mother. The earth is sacred, and so is every step that you take on her. The bowl of the pipe is of red stone; it is the earth. Carved into it and facing the center is the buffalo calf, who stands for all the four-leggeds. The stem is of wood, which stands for all that grows on the earth. These twelve hanging feathers from the Spotted Eagle stand for all the winged creatures. All these living things of the universe are the children of Mother Earth. You are all joined as one family, and you will be reminded of this when you smoke the pipe. Treat this pipe and the earth with respect, and your people will increase and prosper.'

The woman told them that seven circles carved on the stone represented the seven rites in which the people would learn to use the sacred pipe. The first was for the rite of 'keeping the soul', which she now taught them. The remaining rites they would learn in due course.

The woman made as if to leave the lodge, but then she turned and spoke to Standing Hollow Horn again. 'This pipe will carry you to the end. Remember that in me there are four ages. I am going now, but I will look on your people in every age, and at the end I will return.'

She now walked slowly around the lodge in a sunwise direction. The people were silent and filled with awe. Even the hungry young children watched her, their eyes alive with wonder. Then she left. But after she had walked a short distance, she faced the people again and sat down on the prairie. The people gazing after her were amazed to see that when she stood up, she had become a young red and brown buffalo calf. The calf walked further into the prairie, and then lay down and rolled over, looking back at the people.

When she stood up, she was a white buffalo. The white buffalo walked on until she was a bright speck in the distant prairie, and then rolled over again, and became a black buffalo. This buffalo walked away, stopped, bowed to the four directions of the earth, and finally disappeared over the hill.

Coyote and Porcupine

A Nez Perce Legend

Once Porcupine was going along the river bank looking for food. Soon he saw some fine, fat buffalo, ten of them, just across the river. Then Porcupine wanted to get across the river, but could not. After some thought he called to the buffalo to stand in line. This was so that he could tell which one was the fattest. Then he picked out the fattest one and told him to swim across the river. When this buffalo came up to Porcupine, he asked Porcupine where he wanted to sit, on his back or on his tail. Porcupine answered, "I would rather be under your forelegs, so I shall not drown."

The buffalo agreed. When they were nearly across, Porcupine struck the buffalo under the foreleg with a large knife. So, he killed that buffalo, but the others ran away.

Porcupine was looking for something with which to sharpen his knife. He was singing, "I wish I could find something with which to sharpen my knife, for I haven't had any fat buffalo yet." Now, Coyote happened to be going by and he heard Porcupine singing. Coyote came up to him and Porcupine was afraid. Coyote asked him what he was singing, and Porcupine answered, "I was not singing anything, I was just saying I wish I had some string for my moccasin." Coyote said, "No, you did not say that; I heard what you said." Porcupine said nothing more; so, Coyote told him what he had killed. Coyote said, "Now, I have a sharp knife, so I can help you." Then Coyote said, "Let us try jumping over the buffalo; the one who jumps over may have it all. I'll try first." Coyote succeeded, but Porcupine did not, so Coyote got all the meat. Then Coyote took his sharp knife and cut Porcupine's head, but did not kill him.

Now, Coyote had some children: one of them was with him, and the rest were at home. Coyote said to his child, "I am going after the other children. You watch the old Porcupine, and if he gets up you call me and I will come back and kill him." When Coyote was gone, Porcupine got up. The young Coyote cried, "Father, Porcupine is up." Then Coyote hurried back and asked his baby what the matter was. The child said, "He was trying to take some of the buffalo meat, but now he is quiet again." Coyote started off a second time.

When he was a great way off Porcupine got up. The child called his father, but this time in vain. Porcupine struck the young Coyote with a stone and killed him. Then he set the child up under a tree and stuffed his mouth full of buffalo fat. Then Porcupine took all the meat to the top of a tree and watched for Coyote and his family to come.

When Coyote with his wife and children had come up close, Coyote said to the children, "Look at your brother; he is eating and having a great time." But when they arrived, they saw that the baby was killed and had his mouth stuffed with fat. Then Coyote was very angry. He wondered where Porcupine had gone. When Coyote looked up, he saw Porcupine sitting in a tall tree laughing. Coyote said, "Please come down"; but Porcupine answered, "I do not like you because you are trying to cheat me out of my buffalo meat." Coyote said, "Just give us a little piece of fat or meat." Then Porcupine told Coyote and his family to all stand together under the tree. They did this. Then Porcupine dropped the buffalo head down on them and they were all killed.

Coyote Frees the Buffalo

Coyote and his family were living for a long time in a village near the plains that were his hunting grounds. The hunting was good, for there were many buffalo, but one summer, there were none. Coyote and the other hunters traveled for many miles and found not one. Everyone in the village grew thin with hunger. Coyote's children cried because their bellies were empty.

"The buffalo are somewhere," Coyote said to himself. So, the next morning, and the morning after that, and the morning after that, he went out looking. "Somewhere I shall find the buffalo," he told himself each morning. "Why is it that I cannot?"

One day he did not go out onto the planes, but into the woods. Deep in the woods he climbed to the top of a knoll. A wind was blowing there, and in the wind, Coyote smelled meat. He stood still and sniffed again. Yes, meat! Buffalo meat! Coyote lifted his nose and followed the smell. He followed it for miles, up and down, across creeks, and through brambles and brush. This smell grew stronger and stronger until he came at last to a lodge that stood by itself at the edge of a wood. Beyond the wood a high bluff rose above the trees.

Coyote's nose told him that the meat was nearby, but it told him, too, that this was a bad place, so he hid in the bushes and watched. Soon he saw a small child come out of the lodge to play. The child ran all around the lodge. He threw stones at a tree. At last, he went to sit in the doorway of the lodge and deep in the earth with a stick.

Coyote grinned, and turned himself into a small, fat puppy. His coat was brown and black and silky. His eyes and nose were soft. But he forgot to change his whiskers and his eyes. He gave a little yipping bark, and tumbled out of his hiding place.

The little boy looked up and saw him. "Puppy!" he cried. "Puppy come!" And he ran toward Coyote-Pup and took him in his arms. "Father!" he cried as he ran into the lodge. "Father, look! I found a puppy!"

Crow, who was his father, looked at Coyote-Pup and frowned. "That is not a pup. Something is different about it. Something wrong."

"No! It is a puppy!" The child held Coyote-Pup closer.

"No, it is something different, not a real pup," Crow said. "It will be dark soon. Take it out and put it where you found it."

"I will not! It is my puppy. I want to keep it!"

His father frowned. "You cannot. Take it out."

"I won't!"

"Hoh! You will not? Well then, bring it here. We will see whether it is a pup or not," Crow said. He held Coyote-Pup out toward the cook fire and, as it came close to the flames, the pup gave a yip, and wriggled, and made water into the fire.

"Ha!" Crow laughed. "It is a pup! Take him and give him some meat to eat."

So, the child did, and Coyote-Pup ate it all up and begged for more. Later, after dark, when the fire had burned down to coals, Crowe and his son went to their beds, and Coyote-Pup curled up beside the fire. The others soon fell asleep, but Coyote listened, and only pretended to sleep. When it was safe, he turned back into his own shape, slipped out the door, and followed his nose into the night.

His nose led him through the moonlight to the bluff behind the trees behind the lodge. The bluff looked like solid rock, but Coyote's nose told him that there was an opening. He sniffed and sniffed until he came to a crack. He followed the crack. A door. There was a door. He pushed, but it was closed fast. He could find no handle to pull. "Poh!" he said. "Open yourself!"

And the door opened itself.

"Ee-ow!" Coyote yelped and jumped out of the way just in time. A big bull buffalo charged out through the door, and after him thundered cows and bulls and calves, herds of them, and often buffalo to people all of the plains. Coyote danced up and down and urged, "Go, go, go!" as they passed. When the last of the buffalo had run out, Coyote pushed the door shut and hurried after them as they spread out and away toward the plains.

Inside the lodge, Crow woke and heard the thunder of hooves. "Buffalo going by," he thought sleepily. "It is good that all miners shut up." But he was uneasy, and he rose to go out and make sure. When he came to the rocky bluff, he opened the rock door, saw that the caverns were empty, and shouted out to his son, "They are all gone! I knew that pup was no pup!"

When coyote reached his own village, he called out, "Hoh, everyone! I, Coyote, have brought buffalo for our hunters to hunt. Take up your bows and arrows, and go after them!"

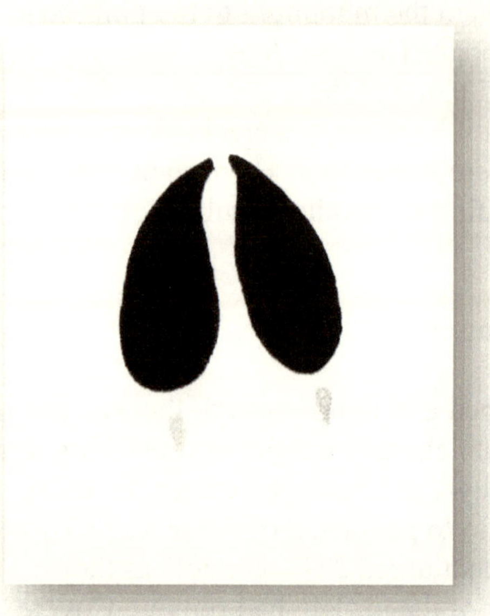

Tale of Coyote Becomes a Buffalo

Dorsey, George A. Traditions of the Caddo. Washington: Carnegie Institution. 1905.

While Coyote was out hunting something to eat, he met Buffalo, who was very powerful among his tribe. He was eating grass and looked fat and well fed. Coyote asked him if he would give him power to turn into a Buffalo and eat grass as he did.

Buffalo said: "Yes, I will give you the power which was given to me by the Great-Father-Above, but when I give you the power you must not use it every chance you get, but only when very necessary." He told Coyote to stand facing the other way and not to move, but to be brave as he was.

Coyote stood still, wondering what was going to happen to him. Buffalo began to throw up dirt with his hoofs and to act very angrily. He told Coyote to keep his eyes closed. Then he made a plunge toward him, and when he was about to strike him with his horns, Coyote jumped out of the way, and Buffalo passed him without touching him. He did this the second, third, fourth, fifth, and sixth times, but the seventh time he stood there without moving. He could hear Buffalo coming at him, but he stood there awaiting what would happen to him. Buffalo struck him and rolled him under his stomach with his horns and threw him up into the air. When he came down on his feet he was turned into a very young Buffalo.

He began to eat green grass at once. Then the old Buffalo told him that if he wanted to turn into a Coyote again, he must find a Buffalo wallow, roll himself over two or three times, and then he would arise a Coyote. Again, Buffalo cautioned him not to use his power too often, telling him that the power was good for only seven times, and he also told him that he must not give the power to any one else, especially to any of his own race.

Before they parted the real Buffalo told Coyote to change back into a Coyote, and he did so, and then they both went on their way. Before Coyote had gone far from Buffalo, he wanted to try his power to see if he could use it alone. He did, and became a Buffalo. During that same day he tried his power three or four times, and before he had met any one, he had tried it six times, and had turned himself into a Buffalo for the seventh time.

While he was a Buffalo, he met one of his own people, a famous Coyote, and so he went up to him and said: "Do not you want me to give you some of my power, so that you can eat grass as I do? You look as though you were very hungry." "Yes," said Coyote. "Well, all right," said Coyote-Buffalo. "Go off a short distance from me and stand there and face the other way. Do not run, but be brave as I am. Close your eyes. Now, I am ready," and so he started at him, but the other Coyote jumped out of the way every time until the last time came. Then Coyote stood his ground, and Coyote-Buffalo rolled him under his stomach, and they both went up in the air and came down on their feet. They were both Coyotes, and they stood looking at each other for a time; then they separated and went off.

The Ghosts' Buffalo

A Blackfoot Legend

A long time ago there were four Blackfeet, who went to war against the Crees. They traveled a long way, and at last their horses gave out, and they started back toward their homes. As they were going along, they came to the Sand Hills; and while they were passing through them, they saw in the sand a fresh travois trail, where people had been travelling.

One of the men said: "Let us follow this trail until we come up with some of our people. Then we will camp with them." They followed the trail for a long way, and at length one of the Blackfeet, named E-kus'-kini, a very powerful person, said to the others: "Why follow this longer? It is just nothing." The others said: "Not so. These are our people. We will go on and camp with them." They went on, and toward evening, one of them found a stone maul and a dog travois. He said: "Look at these things. I know this maul and this travois. They belonged to my mother, who died. They were buried with her. This is strange." He took the things. When night overtook the men, they camped.

Early in the morning, they heard, all about them, sounds as if a camp of people were there. They heard a young man shouting a sort of war cry, as young men do; women chopping wood; a man calling for a feast, asking people to come to his lodge and smoke, all the different sounds of the camp. They looked about, but could see nothing; and then they were frightened and covered their heads with their robes. At last, they took courage, and started to look around and see what they could learn about this strange thing. For a little while they saw nothing, but pretty soon one of them said: "Look over there. See that pis'kun. Let us go over and look at it." As they were going toward it, one of them picked up a stone pointed arrow. He said: "Look at this. It belonged to my father. This is his place." They started to go on toward the pis'kun, but suddenly they could see no pis'kun. It had disappeared all at once.

A little while after this, one of them spoke up, and said: "Look over there. There is my father running buffalo. There! he has killed. Let us go over to him." They all looked where this man pointed, and they could see a person on a white horse, running buffalo. While they were looking, the person killed the buffalo, and got off his horse to butcher it. They started to go over toward him, and saw him at work butchering, and saw him turn the buffalo over on its back; but before they got to the place where he was, the person got on his horse and rode off, and when they got to where he had been skinning the buffalo, they saw lying on the ground only a dead mouse. There was no buffalo there. By the side of the mouse was a buffalo chip, and lying on it was an arrow painted red. The man said: "That is my father's arrow. That is the way he painted them." He took it up in his hands; and when he held it in his hands, he saw that it was not an arrow but a blade of spear grass. Then he laid it down, and it was an arrow again.

Another Blackfoot found a buffalo rock, I-nis'-kim.

Some time after this, the men got home to their camp. The man who had taken the maul and the dog travois, when he got home and smelled the smoke from the fire, died, and so did his horse. It seems that the shadow of the person who owned the things was angry at him and followed him home. Two others of these Blackfeet have since died, killed in war; but E-kus'-kini is alive yet. He took a stone and an iron arrow point that had belonged to his father, and always carried them about with him. That is why he has lived so long. The man who took the stone arrow point found near the pis'kun, which had belonged to his father, took it home with him. This was his medicine. After that he was badly wounded in two fights, but he was not killed; he got well.

The one who took the buffalo rock, I-nis'-kim, it afterward made strong to call the buffalo into the pis'kun. He would take the rock and put it in his lodge close to the fire, where he could look at it, and would pray over it and make medicine. Sometimes he would ask for a hundred buffalo to jump into the pis'kun, and the next day a hundred would jump in. He was powerful.

The Story of the Blood Boy

*Blackfeet Indian
"The Story of
the Blood Boy"
from "Blackfeet
Indian Stories"
by George Bird
Grinnell 1913*

As the children whose ancestors came from Europe have stories about the heroes who killed wicked and cruel monsters—like Jack the Giant Killer, for example—so the Indian children hear stories about persons who had magic power and who went about the world destroying those who treated cruelly or killed the Indians of the camps. Such a hero was Kut-o-yis', and this is how he came to be alive and to travel about from place to place, helping the people and destroying their enemies.

It was long, long ago, down where Two Medicine and Badger Rivers come together, that an old man lived with his wife and three daughters. One day there came to his camp a young man, good-looking, a good hunter, and brave. He stayed in the camp for some time, and whenever he went hunting, he killed game and brought in great loads of meat.

All this time the old man was watching him, for he said in his heart, "This seems a good young man and a good hunter. Perhaps I will give him my daughters for wives, and then he will stay here and help me always."

After a time, the old man decided to do this, and he gave the young man his daughters; and because these three were his only children he gave his son-in-law his dogs and all his property, and for himself and his wife he kept only a little lodge. The young man's wives tanned plenty of cow skins and made a big fine lodge, and in this the son-in-law lived with his wives.

For some time after this the son-in-law was very good and kind to the old people. When he killed any animal he gave them part of the meat, and gave them skins which his mother-in-law tanned for robes or for clothing.

As time went on the son-in-law began to grow stingy, and pretty soon he gave nothing to his father-in-law's lodge, but kept everything for his own.

Now, the son-in-law was a person of much mysterious power, and he kept the buffalo hidden under a big log-jam in the river. Whenever he needed food and wished to kill anything, he would take his father-in-law with him to help. He would send the old man out to stamp on the log-jam and frighten the buffalo, and when they ran out from under it the young man would shoot one or two with his arrows, never killing more than he needed. But often he gave the old people nothing at all to eat. They were hungry all the time, and at length they began to grow thin and weak.

One morning early the young man asked his father-in-law to come and hunt with him. They went to the log-jam and the old man drove out the buffalo and his son-in-law killed a fat buffalo cow. Then he said to his father-in-law, "Hurry back now to the camp and tell your daughters to come and carry home the meat, and then you can have something to eat." The old man set out for the camp, thinking, as he walked along, "Now, at last, my son-in-law has taken pity on me; he will give me some of this meat."

When he returned with his daughters, they skinned the cow and cut it up and, carrying it, swept home. The young man had his wives leave the meat at his own lodge and told his father-in-law to go home. He did not give him even a little piece of the meat. The two older daughters gave their parents nothing to eat, but sometimes the youngest one had pity on them and took a piece of meat and, when she could, threw it into the lodge to the old people. The son-in-law had told his wives not to give the old people anything to eat. Except for the good heart of the youngest daughter, they would have died of hunger.

Another day the son-in-law rose early in the morning and went over to the old man's lodge and kicked against the poles, calling to him, "Get up now and help me; I want you to go and stamp on the log-jam to drive out the buffalo." When the old man moved his feet on the jam and a buffalo ran out, the son-in-law was not ready for it, and it passed by him before he shot the arrow; so, he only wounded it. It ran away, but at last it fell down and died.

The old man followed close after it, and as he ran along, he came to a place where a great clot of blood had fallen from the buffalo's wound. When he came to where this clot of blood was lying on the ground, he stumbled and fell and spilled his arrows out of his quiver, and while he was picking them up, he picked up also the clot of blood and hid it in his quiver.

"What are you picking up?" called the son-in-law.

"Nothing," replied the old man. "I fell down and spilled my arrows, and I am putting them back."

"Ah, old man," said the son-in-law, "you are lazy and useless. You no longer help me. Go back now to the camp and tell your daughters to come down here and help carry in this meat."

The old man went to the camp and told his daughters of the meat that their husband had killed, and they went down to the killing ground. Then he went to his own lodge and said to his wife, "Hurry, now, put the stone kettle on the fire. I have brought home something from the killing."

"Ah," said the old woman, "has our son-in-law been generous and given us something nice to eat?"

"No," replied the old man, "but hurry and put the kettle on the fire.

After a time, the water began to boil and the old man turned his quiver upside down over the pot, and immediately there came from it a sound of a child crying, as if it were being hurt. The old people both looked in the kettle and there they saw a little boy, and they quickly took him out of the water. They were surprised and did not know where the child had come from. The old woman wrapped the child up and wound a line about its wrappings to keep them in place, making a lashing for the child. Then they talked about it, wondering what should be done with it. They thought that if their son-in-law knew it was a boy, he would kill it; so, they determined to tell their daughters that the baby was a girl, for then their son-in-law would think that he was going to have another wife. So, he would be glad. They called the child Kut-o-yis'—Clot of Blood.

The son-in-law and his wives came home, bringing the meat, and after a little time they heard the child in the next lodge crying. The son-in-law said to his youngest wife, "Go over to your mother's and see whether that baby is a boy or a girl. If it is a boy, tell your parents to kill it."

Soon the young woman came back and said to her husband, "It is a girl baby."

The son-in-law did not know whether to believe this, and sent his oldest wife to ask the same question. When she came back and told him the same thing, he believed that it was really a girl. Then he was glad. He said to his youngest wife, "Take some back fat and pemmican over to your mother; she must be well fed now that she has to nurse this child."

On the fourth day after he had been born the child spoke and said to his mother, "Hold me in turn to each one of these lodge poles, and when I come to the last one, I shall fall out of my lashings and be grown up." The old woman did as he had said, and as she held him to one pole after another he could be seen to grow; and finally, when he was held to the last pole, he was a man.

After Kut-o-yis' had looked about the lodge he put his eye to a hole in the lodge-covering and looked out. Then he turned around and said to the old people, "How is it that in this lodge there is nothing to eat? Over by the other lodge I see plenty of food hanging up."

"Hush," said the old woman, raising her hand, "you will be heard. Our son-in-law lives over there. He does not give us anything at all to eat."

"Well," said the young man, "where is your piskun—where do you kill buffalo?"

"It is down by the river," the old woman answered. "We pound on it and the buffalo run out."

For some time, they talked together and thc old man told Kut-o-yis' how his son-in-law had abused him. He said to the young man, "He has taken from me my bow and my arrows and has taken even my dogs; and now for many days we have had nothing to eat, except sometimes a small piece of meat that our daughter throws to us."

"Father," said Kut-o-yis', "have you no arrows?"

"No, my son," replied the old man, "but I still have four stone arrow points."

"Go out then," said Kut-o-yis', "and get some wood. We will make a bow and some arrows, and in the morning, we will go down to where the buffalo are and kill something to eat."

Early in the morning Kut-o-yls' pushed the old man and said, "Come, get up now, and we will go down and kill, when the buffalo come out." It was still very early in the morning.

When they reached the river the old man said, "This is the place to stand and shoot. I will go down and drive them out."

He went down and stamped on the log-jam, and presently a fat cow ran out and Kut-o-yis' killed it.

Now, after these two had gone to the river the son-in-law arose and went over to the old man's lodge, and knocked on the poles and called to the old man to get up and help him kill. The old woman called out to the son-in-law, saying, "Your father-in-law has already gone down to the piskun." This made the son-in-law angry, and he began to talk badly to the old woman and to threaten to harm her.

Presently he went on down to the log-jam, and as he got near the place he saw the old man at work there, bending over, skinning a buffalo; for Kut-o-yis', when he had seen the son-in-law coming, had lain down on the ground and hidden himself behind the carcass.

When the son-in-law had come pretty close to where the buffalo lay, he said to his father-in-law, "Old man, stand up and look everything about you. Look carefully and well, for it will be the last time that you will ever see anything"; and while the son-in-law said this, he took an arrow from his quiver.

Kut-o-yis' spoke to the old man from his hiding-place and said, "Tell your son-in-law that he must take his last look, for that you are going to kill him now." The old man said this as he had been told.

"Ah," said the son-in-law, "you talk back to me. That makes me still angrier at you." He put an arrow on the string and shot at the old man, but did not hit him. Kut-o-yis' said to the old man, "Pick up that arrow and shoot it back at him"; and the old man did so. Now, they shot at each other four times, and then the old man said to Kut-o-yis', "I am afraid now; get up and help me. If you do not, I think he will kill me." Then Kut-o-yis' rose to his feet and said to the son-in-law, "Here, what are you doing? I think you have been treating this old man badly for a long time. Why do you do it?"

"Oh no," said the son-in-law, and he smiled at Kut-o-yis' in a friendly way, for he was afraid of him. "Oh no; no one thinks more of this old man than I do. I have always been very good to him."

"No," said Kut-o-yis'. "You are saying what is not true, and I am going to kill you now."

Kut-o-yis' shot the son-in-law four times and he fell down and died. Then the young man told his father to go and bring down to him the daughters who had acted badly toward him. The old man did so and Kut-o-yis' punished them. Then he went up to the lodges and said to the youngest woman, "Did you love your husband?" "Yes," said the girl, "I loved him." So Kut-o-yis' punished her too, but not so badly as he had the other daughters, because she had been kind to her parents.

To the old people he said, "Go over now to that lodge and live there. There is plenty of food, and when that is gone, I will kill more. As for me, I shall make a journey. Tell me where there are any people. In what direction shall I go to find a camp?"

"Well," said the old man, "up here on Two Medicine Lodge Creek there are some people—up where the piskun is, you know."

Kut-o-yis' followed up the stream to where the piskun was and there found many lodges of people. In the center of the camp was a big lodge, and painted on it the figure of a bear. He did not go to this lodge, but went into a small lodge where two old women lived. When he had sat down, they put food before him—lean dried meat and some belly fat.

"How is this, grandmothers?" he said. "Here is a camp with plenty of fat meat and back fat hanging up to dry; why do you not give me some of that?"

"Hush; be careful," said the old women. "In that big lodge over there lives a big bear and his wives and children. He takes all the best food and leaves us nothing. He is the chief of this place."

Early in the morning Kut-o-yis' said to the old women, "Harness up your dogs to the travois now and go over to the piskun, and I will kill some fat meat for you."

When they got there, he killed a fat cow and helped the old women to cut it up, and they took it to the lodge. One of those old women said, "Ah me, the bears will be sure to come."

"Why do you say that?" he asked.

They said to him, "We shall be sorry to lose this back fat."

"Do not fear," he said. "No one shall take this back fat from you. Now, take all those best pieces and hang them up, so that those who live in the bear lodge may see them."

They did so. Pretty soon the old bear chief said to one of his children, "By this time I think the people have finished killing. Go out now and look about; see where the nicest pieces are, and bring in some nice back fat."

One of the young bears went out of the lodge and stood up and looked about, and when it saw this meat hanging by the old women's lodge close by, it went over toward it.

"Ah," said the old women, "there are those bears."
"Do not be afraid," said Kut-o-yis'.

The young bear went over to where the meat was hanging and stood up and began to pull it down. Kut-o-yis' went out of the lodge and said, "Wait; wait! What are you doing, taking the old women's meat?"

The young bear answered, "My father told me that I should go out and get this meat and bring it home to him."

Kut-o-yis' hit the young bear over the head with a stick and it ran home crying.

When it had reached the lodge, it told what had happened and the father bear said, "I will go over there myself; perhaps this person will hit me over the head."

When the old women saw the father and mother bear and all their relations coming, they were afraid, but Kut-o-yis' jumped out of the lodge and killed the bears one after another; all except one little she-bear, a very small one, which got away.

"Well," said Kut-o-yis', "you may go and breed more bears."

He told the old women to move over to the bear-painted lodge and after this to live in it. It was theirs.

To the old women Kut-o-yis' then said, "Now, grandmothers, where are there any more people? I want to travel about and see them."

The old women said, "At the Point of Rocks —on Sun River—there is a camp. There is a piskun there."

So Kut-o-yis' set off for that place, and when he came to the camp he went into an old woman's lodge.

The old woman gave him something to eat—a dish of bad food.

"Why is this, grandmother?" asked Kut-o-yis'. "Have you no food better than this to give to a visitor? Down there I see a piskun; you must kill plenty of buffalo and must have good food."

"Speak lower," said the old woman, "or you may be heard. We have no good food because there is a great snake here who is the chief of the camp. He takes all the best pieces. He lives over there in that snake-painted lodge."

The next morning when the buffalo were led in, Kut-o-yis' killed one, and they took the back fat and carried it to their lodge. Then Kut-o-yis' said, "I think I will visit that snake per-son." He went over and went into the lodge, and there he saw many women that the snake person had taken to be his wives. The women were cooking some service berries. Kut-o-yis' picked up the dish and ate the berries and threw the dish away. Then he went up to the big snake, who was lying there asleep, and pricked him with his knife, saying, "Here, get up; I have come to visit you. Let us smoke together."

Then the snake was angry and he raised up his head and began to rattle, and Kut-o-yis' cut off his head and cut him in pieces. He cut off the heads of all the snake's wives and children; all except one little female snake which got away by crawling into a crack in the rocks.

"Oh, well," said Kut-o-yis', "you can go and breed snakes so there will be more. The people will not be afraid of little snakes."

Kut-o-yis' said to the old woman, "Now, grandmother, go into this snake lodge and take it for your own and everything that is in it."

Then he said to them, "Where are there some more people?" They told him there were some camps down the river and some up in the mountains, but they said, "Do not go up there. It is bad because there lives Ai-sin'-o-ko-ki—Wind Sucker. He will kill you."

Kut-o-yis' was glad to know that there was such a person, and he went to the mountains. When he reached the place where Wind Sucker lived, he looked into his mouth and saw there many dead people. Some were skeletons and some had only just died. He went in, and there he saw a fearful sight. The ground was white as snow with the bones of those who had died. There were bodies with flesh on them; some who had died not long before and some who were still living.

As he looked about, he saw hanging down above him a great thing that seemed to move—to grow a little larger and then to grow a little smaller.

Kut-o-yis' spoke to one of the people who was alive and asked, "What is that hanging down above us?"

The person answered him, "That is Wind Sucker's heart."

Then Kut-o-yis' spoke to all the living and said to them, "You who still draw a little breath try to move your heads in time to the song that I shall sing; and you who are still able to move stand up on your feet and dance. Take courage now; we are going to dance to the ghosts."

Then Kut-o-yis' tied his knife, point upward, to the top of his head and began to dance, singing the ghost song, and all the others danced with him; and as he danced up and down, he kept springing higher and higher into the air, and the point of his knife cut Wind Sucker's heart and killed him.

Then Kut-o-yis', with his knife, cut a hole between Wind Sucker's ribs, and he and all those who were able to move crawled out through the hole. He said to those who could still walk that they should go and tell their people to come here, to get the ones still alive but unable to travel.

To some of these people that he had freed he said, "Where are there any other people? I want to visit all the people."

"There is a camp to the westward, up the river," they replied; "but you must not take the left-hand trail going up because on that trail lives a woman who invites men to wrestle with her and then kills them. Avoid her."

Now, really, this was what Kut-o-yis' was looking for. This was what he was doing in the world, trying to kill off all the bad things. He, asked these people just where this woman lived and how it was best for him to go so that he should not meet her. He did this because he did not wish the people to know that he was going where she was.

He started, and after he had travelled some time he saw a woman standing not far from the trail. She called to him, saying, "Come here, young man, come here; I want to wrestle with you."

"No," he replied, "I am in a hurry; I can-not stop."
The woman called again, "No, no; do not go on; come now and wrestle once with me."

After she had called him the fourth time, Kut-o-yis' went to her.

Now on the ground where this woman wrestled with people, she had placed many sharp, broken flint-stones, partly hiding them by the grass. The two seized each other and began to wrestle over these sharp stones, but Kut-o-yis' looked at the ground and did not step on them. He watched his chance and gave the woman a quick wrench, and threw her down on a, large sharp flint which cut her in two; and the parts of her body fell asunder.

Kut-o-yis' then went on, and after a time came to where a woman had made a place for sliding downhill. At the far end of it she had fixed a rope which, when she raised it, would trip people up, and when they were tripped, they fell over a high cliff into a deep water, where a great fish ate them.

When this woman saw Kut-o-yis' coming she cried out to him, "Come over here, young man, and slide with me."

"No," he replied, "I am in a hurry; I cannot wait." She kept calling to him, and when she had called him the fourth time he went over where he was to slide with her.

"This sliding," said the woman, "is very good fun."

"Ah, yes," said Kut-o-yis', "I will look at it."

As he went near the place he looked carefully and saw the hidden rope. He began to slide, and holding his knife in his hand, when he reached the rope, he cut it just as the woman raised it and pulled on it, and the woman fell over backward into the water and was eaten up by the big fish.

From here he went on again, and after a time he came to a big camp. A man-eater was the chief of this place.

Before Kut-o-yis' went to the chief's lodge he looked about and saw a little girl and called her to him and said, "Child, I am going into that lodge, to let that man-eater kill and eat me. Therefore, be on the watch, and if you can get hold of one of my bones take it out and call all the dogs to you, and when they have come to you throw down the bone and say, Kut-o-yis', the dogs are eating your bones."

Then Kut-o-yis' entered the lodge, and when the man-eater saw him, he called out, "Oki, oki!" (Welcome, welcome!) and seemed glad to see him, for he was a fat young man. The man-eater took a knife and walked up to Kut-o-yis' and cut his throat and put him into a great stone pot to cook. When the meat was cooked, he pulled the kettle from the fire and ate the body, limb by limb, until it was all eaten.

After that the little girl who was watching came into the lodge and said, "Pity me, man-eater, my mother is hungry and asks you for those bones." The old man gathered them together and handed them to her, and she took them out of the lodge. When she had gone a little way, she called all the dogs to her and threw down the bones to the dogs, crying out, "Look out, Kut-o-yis', the dogs are eating you," and when she said that, Kut-o-yis' arose from the pile of bones.

Again, he went into the lodge, and when the man-eater saw him, he cried out, "How, how, how! the fat young man has survived!" and he seemed surprised. Again, he took his knife and cut the throat of Kut-o-yis' and threw him into the kettle. Again, when the meat was cooked, he ate it, and when the little girl asked for the bones again, he gave them to her. She took them out and threw them to the dogs, crying, "Kut-o-yis', the dogs are eating you," and again Kut-o-yis' arose from the bones.

When the man-eater had cooked him four times Kut-o-yis' again went into the lodge, and seizing the man-eater, he threw him into the boiling kettle, and his wives and all his children, and boiled them.

The man-eater was the seventh and last of the bad things to be destroyed by Kut-o-yis'.

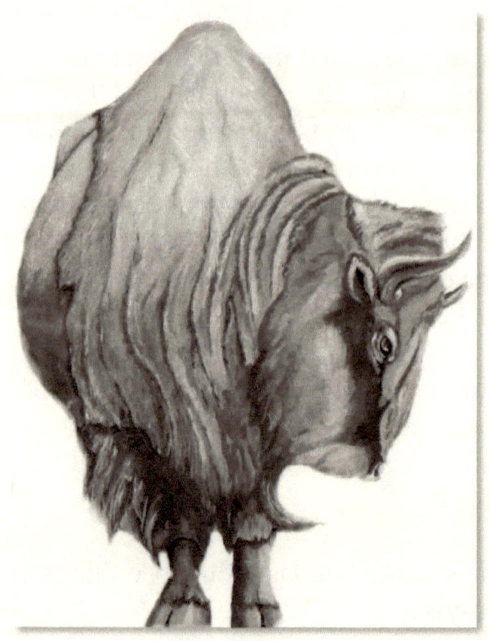

Myth of the White Buffalo Woman

*Sioux
(From Edward S. Curtis, The North American Indian, Vol. 3 (1908), pp. 56-60)*

Many generations ago, when the Lakota still dwelt beside the lake far away in the east, they experienced a winter of terrible severity. The snow lay deep on the ground, and the streams were frozen to their very beds. Every day could be heard the sharp crack of trees as the frost gnawed at their hearts; and at night the piles of skins and the blazing fires in the teepees scarcely sufficed to keep the blood coursing through the veins. Game seemed to have deserted the country, for though the hunters often faced the hardships of the winter chase, they returned empty-handed, and the wail of hungry women and children joined with the moan of the forest. When finally, a tardy spring arrived, it was decided to leave a country so exposed to the anger of Wazíya, Spirit of the North, and seek a better homeland in the direction of the sunset, where ruled the Wing Flappers, who existed from the beginning.

There was little enough to pack besides teepees and fur robes, and what few dogs had not been eaten were soon harnessed to the laden travois. Two young men were sent in advance. No pair could have been more different in their nature than these two, for while one was brave, chivalrous, unselfish, and kind, the other's heart was bad, and he thought only of the sensuous and vicious.

Unencumbered as they were, the scouts were soon far ahead of the wearily dragging line of haggard men, women bent under burdens that dogs should have been drawing, straggling children, and a few gaunt dogs tugging at the over laden travois. Late in the day the scouts succeeded in shooting a deer, and thinking their people would reach that point for the night's camp, they left it where it had fallen and were turning away to seek other game when one of them felt a sudden impulse to look back. Wonderful sight! There in a mist that rose above a little hill appeared the outline of a woman. As they gazed in astonishment, the cloud slowly lifted, and the young men saw that she was a maiden fair and beautiful. Her only dress was a short skirt, wristlets, and anklets, all of sage. In the crook of her left arm, she carried a bundle wrapped closely in a red buffalo-skin; on her back was a quiver, and in her left hand she held a bunch of herbs. Straightway the young man whose heart was evil was overpowered by a desire to possess the beautiful woman, but his companion endeavored to dissuade him with the caution that she might be . . . a messenger from the Great Mystery.

"No, no!" he cried vehemently, "she is not holy, but a woman, human like ourselves, and I will have her!"

Without waiting he ran toward the woman, who forthwith warned him that she was a sacred being. When he persisted and went closer, she commanded him sternly to stop, for his heart was evil and he was unworthy to come near to the holy things she bore. As he still advanced, she retreated, laid her burden on the ground, and then came toward him. Suddenly it appeared to the waiting youth that the mist descended and enveloped the mysterious woman and his companion. Then followed a fearful sound of rattling and hissing as of thousands of angered rattlesnakes. The terrified observer was about to flee from the dreadful place when the cloud lifted as suddenly as it had descended, disclosing the bleached bones of his former comrade, and the beautiful virgin standing calmly beside them. She spoke to him gently, bidding him have no fear, for he was chosen to be priest of his nation.

"I have many things to impart to your people," she said. "Go now to the place where they are encamped, and bid them prepare for my coming. Build a great circle of green boughs, leaving an opening at the east. In the center erect a council teepee, and over the ground inside spread sage thickly. In the morning I shall come."

Filled with awe, the young man hastened back and delivered to his people the message of the holy woman. Under his direction her commands were reverently obeyed, for were they not a message from the Great Mystery? In the morning, gathered within the circle of green boughs, they waited in great expectancy, looking for the messenger of the Mystery to enter through the opening left at the east. Suddenly, obeying a common impulse, they turned and looked in the opposite direction, and behold! she stood before them.

Entering the teepee with a number of just and upright men selected by the youth whom she had chosen to receive the sacred rites, she at once spread open the red buffalo-skin, exposing its contents--tobacco, the feather of a spotted eagle, the skin of a red-headed woodpecker, a roll of buffalo-hair, a few braids of sweet-grass, and, chief of all, a red stone pipe with the carved image of a buffalo calf surmounting its wooden stem. At the same time, she explained that the Great Mystery had sent her to reveal to them his laws, and teach them how to worship, that they might become a great and powerful people.

During the four days she remained with them in the teepee she instructed them in the customs they were to observe-- how the man who would have great [spiritual] power should go into the high places and fast for many days, when he would see visions and obtain strength from the Mysteries; how to punish him of evil heart who sinned against the rights of his brother; how to instruct girls at maturity, and to care for the sick. She taught them also how to worship the Great Mystery. . ..

Then she taught them carefully the five great ceremonies they were to observe: . . . the Foster-parent Chant, the Sun Dance, the Vision Cry, the Buffalo Chant, and the Ghost Keeper. The sacred pipe she gave into the keeping of the chosen young man, with the admonition that its wrapping should be removed only in cases of direst tribal necessity. From the quiver on her back she took six bows and six arrows, and distributed them among as many young men, renowned for their bravery, hospitality, and truthfulness. These weapons she bade them take, after her departure, to the summit of a certain hill, where they would find a herd of six hundred buffalo, all of which they were to kill. In the midst of the herd would be found six men. These also they were to kill, then cut off their ears and attach them to the stem of the sacred pipe. Her last words were these:

"So long as you believe in this pipe and worship the Mystery as I have taught you, so long will you prosper; you will have food in plenty; you will increase and be powerful as a nation. But when you, as a people, cease to reverence the pipe, then will you cease to be a nation."

With these words she left the teepee and went to the opening at the eastern side of the camp-circle. Suddenly she disappeared, and the people, crowding forward to see what had become of her, beheld only a white buffalo cow trotting over the prairie.

Yellowstone Valley and the Great Flood

Cheyenne

He was an old Indian. His face was weather beaten, but his eyes were still bright. I never knew what tribe he was from, though I could guess. Yet others from the tribe whom I talked to later had never heard his story.

We had been talking of the visions of the young men. He sat for a long time, looking out across the Yellowstone Valley through the pouring rain, before he spoke. "They are beginning to come back," he said.

"Who is coming back?" I asked.

"The animals," he said. "It has happened before."

"Tell me about it.'

He thought for a long while before he lifted his hands and his eyes. "The Great Spirit smiled on this land when he made it. There were mountains and plains, forests and grasslands. There were animals of many kinds--and men."

The old man's hands moved smoothly, telling the story more clearly than his voice.

The Great Spirit told the people, "These animals are your brothers. Share the land with them. They will give you food and clothing. Live with them and protect them.

"Protect especially the buffalo, for the buffalo will give you food and shelter. The hide of the buffalo will keep you from the cold, from the heat, and from the rain. As long as you have the buffalo, you will never need to suffer."

For many winters the people lived at peace with the animals and with the land. When they killed a buffalo, they thanked the Great Spirit, and they used every part of the buffalo. It took care of every need.

Then other people came. They did not think of the animals as brothers. They killed, even when they did not need food. They burned and cut the forests, and the animals died. They shot the buffalo and called it sport. They killed the fish in the streams.

When the Great Spirit looked down, he was sad. He let the smoke of the fires lie in the valleys. The people coughed and choked. But still they burned and they killed.

So, the Great Spirit sent rains to put out the fires and to destroy the people.

The rains fell, and the waters rose. The people moved from the flooded valleys to the higher land.

Spotted Bear, the medicine man, gathered together his people. He said to them, "The Great Spirit has told us that as long as we have the buffalo, we will be safe from heat and cold and rain. But there are no longer any buffalo. Unless we can find buffalo and live at peace with nature, we will all die."

Still the rains fell, and the waters rose. The people moved from the flooded plains to the hills.

The young men went out and hunted for the buffalo. As they went, they put out the fires. They made friends with the animals once more. They cleaned out the streams.

Still the rains fell, and the waters rose. The people moved from the flooded hills to the mountains.

Two young men came to Spotted Bear. "We have found the buffalo," they said. "There was a cow, a calf, and a great white bull. The cow and the calf climbed up to the safety of the mountains. They should be back when the rain stops. But the bank gave way, and the bull was swept away by the floodwaters. We followed and got him to shore, but he had drowned. We have brought you his hide."

They unfolded a huge white buffalo skin.

Spotted Bear took the white buffalo hide. "Many people have been drowned," he said. "Our food has been carried away. But our young people are no longer destroying the world that was created for them. They have found the white buffalo. It will save those who are left."

Still the rains fell, and the waters rose. The people moved from the flooded mountains to the highest peaks.

Spotted Bear spread the white buffalo skin on the ground. He and the other medicine men scraped it and stretched it, and scraped it and stretched it.

Still the rains fell. Like all rawhide, the buffalo skin stretched when it was wet. Spotted Bear stretched it out over the village. All the people who were left crowded under it.

As the rains fell, the medicine men stretched the buffalo skin across the mountains. Each day they stretched it farther.

Then Spotted Bear tied one corner to the top of the Big Horn Mountains. That side, he fastened to the Pryors. The next corner he tied to the Bear Tooth Mountains. Crossing the Yellowstone Valley, he tied one corner to the Crazy Mountains, and the other to Signal Butte in the Bull Mountains.

The whole Yellowstone Valley was covered by the white buffalo skin. Though the rains still fell above, it did not fall in the Yellowstone Valley.

The waters sank away. Animals from the outside moved into the valley, under the white buffalo skin. The people shared the valley with them.

Still the rains fell above the buffalo skin. The skin stretched and began to sag.

Spotted Bear stood on the Bridger Mountains and raised the west end of the buffalo skin to catch the West Wind. The West Wind rushed in and was caught under the buffalo skin. The wind lifted the skin until it formed a great dome over the valley.

The Great Spirit saw that the people were living at peace with the earth. The rains stopped, and the sun shone. As the sun shone on the white buffalo skin, it gleamed with colors of red and yellow and blue.

As the sun shone on the rawhide, it began to shrink. The ends of the dome shrank away until all that was left was one great arch across the valley.

The old man's voice faded away; but his hands said "Look," and his arms moved toward the valley.

The rain had stopped and a rainbow arched across the Yellowstone Valley. A buffalo calf and its mother grazed beneath it.

How the Buffalo were Released on Earth

In the first days a powerful being named Humpback owned all the buffalo. He kept them in a corral in the mountains north of San Juan, where he lived with his young son. Not one buffalo would Humpback release for the people on earth, nor would he share any meat with those who lived near him.

Coyote decided that something should be done to release the buffalo from Humpback's corral. He called the people to a council. "Humpback will not give us any buffalo," Coyote said. "Let us all go over to his corral and make a plan to release them."

They camped in the mountains near Humpback's place, and after dark they made a careful inspection of his buffalo enclosure. The stone walls were too high to climb, and the only entrance was through the back door of Humpback's house.

After four days Coyote summoned the people to another council, and asked them to offer suggestions for releasing the buffalo. "There is no way," said one man. "To release the buffalo, we must go into Humpback's house, and he is too powerful a being for us to do that."

"I have a plan," Coyote said. "For four days we have secretly watched Humpback and his young son go about their daily activities. Have you not observed that the boy does not own a pet of any kind?"

The people did not understand what this had to do with releasing the buffalo, but they knew that Coyote was a great schemer and they waited for him to explain. "I shall change myself into a killdeer," Coyote said. "In the morning when Humpback's son goes down to the spring to get water, he will find a killdeer with a broken wing. He will want this bird for a pet and will take it back into the house. Once I am in the house I can fly into the corral, and the cries of a killdeer will frighten the buffalo into a stampede. They will come charging out through Humpback's house and be released upon the earth."

The people thought this was a good plan, and the next Morning when Humpback's son came down the path to the spring, he found a killdeer with a crippled wing. As Coyote had foreseen, the boy picked up the bird and carried it into the house.

"Look here," the boy cried. "This is a very good bird!"

"It is good for nothing!" Humpback shouted. "All the birds and animals and people are rascals and schemers." Above his fierce nose Humpback wore a blue mask, and through its slits his eyes glittered. His basket headdress was shaped like a cloud and was painted black with a zig-zag streak of yellow to represent lightning. Buffalo horns protruded from the sides.

"It is a very good bird," the boy repeated.

"Take it back where you found it!" roared Humpback, and his frightened son did as he was told.

As soon as the killdeer was released it returned to where the people were camped and changed back to Coyote. "I have failed," he said, "but that makes no difference. I will try again in the morning. Perhaps a small animal will be better than a bird."

The next morning when Humpback's son went to the spring, he found a small dog there, lapping at the water. The boy picked up the dog at once and hurried back into the house. "Look here!" he cried. "What a nice pet I have."

"How foolish you are, boy!" Humpback growled. "A dog is good for nothing. I'll kill it with my club."

The boy held tight to the dog, and started to run away crying.

"Oh, very well," Humpback said. "But first let me test that animal to make certain it is a dog. All animals in the world are schemers." He took a coal of fire from the hearth and brought it closer and closer to the dog's eyes until it gave three rapid barks. "It is a real dog," Humpback declared. "You may keep it in the buffalo corral, but not in the house."

This of course was exactly what Coyote wanted. As soon as darkness fell and Humpback and his son went to sleep, Coyote opened the back door of the house. Then he ran among the buffalo, barking as loud as he could. The buffalo were badly frightened because they had never before heard a dog bark. When Coyote ran nipping at their heels, they stampeded toward Humpback's house and entered the rear door. The pounding of their hooves awakened Humpback, and although he jumped out of bed and tried to stop them, the buffalo smashed down his front door and escaped.

After the last of the shaggy animals had galloped away, Humpback's son could not find his small dog. "Where is my pet?" he cried. "Where is my little dog?"

"That was no dog," Humpback said sadly. "That was Coyote the Trickster. He has turned loose all our buffalo."

Thus, it was that the buffalo were released to scatter over all the earth.

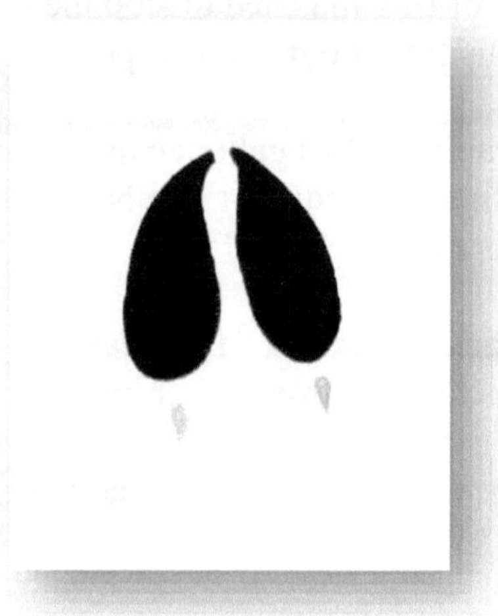

How Medicine Man Resurrected Buffalo

At one time an Arapaho Medicine Man named Black-Robe wanted very much to be able to make magic because his people were very hungry. How could he lure the buffaloes back to the Arapaho hunting grounds? Buffalo meat was their principal food.

Black-Robe decided to ask Cedar-Tree for his help. "Go west and hunt buffalo for our people. Try very hard to find at least one buffalo."

Cedar-Tree hunted hard as he was asked to do. After a long time, he saw some black objects at a distance. "Could they be buffaloes?" he wondered.

Encouraged, he walked faster, but as he drew closer, he was less sure the black objects were buffaloes. Suddenly, he saw the black things fly toward the sky. By then, Cedar-Tree seemed certain the objects were oversized ravens.

Disappointed, he returned to his village, reporting to Black-Robe what he had seen. The Medicine Man scolded him for not believing that what he had seen were buffaloes.

"If you had only believed strong enough, the buffaloes would not have changed to ravens," said Black Robe.

By now the Arapahoes were desperately hungry. One woman on the verge of starving made soup from the soles of her moccasins. The next day her uncle, Trying-Bear, set out early to hunt for anything edible. He had no weapons. Fortunately, on the way he met Black-Robe who loaned him a bow and some arrows.

"Tomorrow morning, I will come to your tent to learn of your success," said Black-Robe. "You must even try to find a dried buffalo, if not a live one."

After hunting a long time to the northwest, Trying-Bear finally found a dried buffalo. He ran home swiftly to tell his people. Black-Robe painted his white pony black and wrapped a black buffalo robe about himself. He stuck his lucky eagle-feather in his hair, mounted his black pony, and took off in a rush to find the dried buffalo.

"Follow me, Trying-Bear," Black-Robe called.

Because he wanted to see what Black-Robe would do with the dried buffalo, Trying-Bear followed rapidly. Medicine Man arrived about midday at the place of the dead buffalo. He dismounted, took aim with his magic eagle-feather, and threw it straight at the carcass. Immediately, a live buffalo jumped to its feet!

Black-Robe turned and saw Trying-Bear. "Shoot it!" commanded Medicine Man. Trying-Bear shot it dead.

"Let's skin it and carry everything eatable back to our people," said Black-Robe.

A feast of thanksgiving and rejoicing followed. Black-Robe had saved his people from starvation. Arapahoes still love to tell this story of how their Medicine Man resurrected the dead buffalo with his magic eagle feather-medicine!

White Crow Hides the Animals

Out on the plains there was a camp where the hunters were never successful. They could not understand this. Every time they went out to hunt, the game scattered and hid where it could not be killed. This caused the people to starve.

The people did not know that there was someone who went out and told all the buffalo and deer within reach that the hunters were coming and to hide. There was a man in camp who could turn himself into a white crow. He went out and told all the animals to make their getaway. This person, White Crow, would come back later in the day when no one could see him and turn himself back into a man.

The starving people moved their camp in various directions trying to find where the game went. White Crow did not move. Under his lodge was a hole where all the buffalo were. This is where he got his food.

When the people returned to one camp, they found this man still living there. He said, "Why did you come back? I have nothing to eat. I have been having just as hard a time as you. I have had nothing to eat since you left."

One day, some of the men were playing a game with sticks and White Crow came toward them. The players smelled the odor of buffalo fat coming from the direction where the man was standing. They noticed that the man had on a good-looking buffalo hide, turned inside out to disguise its newness. He also had a sacred stick rubbed with buffalo fat that they could smell. He did not like their looking at him. He slipped away so they could not ask him questions.

Coyote was there in that village. That night he called the men together and offered to look around White Crow's camp and tell them what he learned. Coyote watched White Crow's camp for a while, the came back and told the men he needed two good men with good eyes. Owl and Dragonfly were the ones chosen. Coyote told them to lie down in the grass and watch White Crow wherever he went. Dragonfly watched so hard, his eyes came out. Owl strained his eyes until they became larger than ordinary eyes. Owl watched the man until he saw him go down in the ground.

When Owl came back, coyote told the men to gather everyone together and announce they were moving camp. Coyote was going to change himself into a little pup and they were to leave him behind. White Crow had a daughter, Coyote told them. "When the people leave, she will search the camp for anything left behind and will find me."

The next day, everyone moved and Coyote turned himself into a dog, but he forgot to put on the whiskers of a dog. The little girl found him and brought him to her lodge. When White Crow came in, he asked to examine the dog. He saw that there were no whiskers and he told his daughter that he was afraid of this. He said it was a person disguised as a dog. But the girl said she wanted to keep it anyway. She refused to throw it away. She gave it a piece of meat while her father went out to warn all the game to be alert.

One day when the man was gone, the little girl removed the stone that covered the buffalo hole. She called the puppy over to look into the hole but he acted as if her were afraid. "Come over here. Look in here pup, see what we have." When she said this, the pup came over. Suddenly he jumped into the hole, and turned into a man and began to holler, "Scatter all over the world! Scatter! Scatter!" The buffalo came out of the ground like a big river. Coyote turned himself into a cocklebur and stuck himself on the fetlock of the last buffalo that go past the girl, who was waiting for him with a club. After the buffalo got out of White Crow's lodge and were a long way off Coyote became a man again and shouted "Scatter! Scatter!"

When White Crow returned to his camp and saw what had happened, he said to the young girl, "See what you have done! I was afraid something like this would happen. Now we are going to have a hard time."

Coyote returned to his people and they began to enjoy the buffalo again. This made White Crow angry. He directed the buffalo and the other animals to hide from the hunters. Soon the people were starving again. White Crow let them know he was going to make it harder than before. He flew over the camp saying, "I want you to know it was me who kept you from killing the buffalo before. You are not going to kill meat animals any more."

That night, Coyote called the men together and told them he had a plan. They would have to follow his instructions carefully. They were to announce that everyone should move over to a forest a few valleys away. Coyote would turn himself into a bull elk and hide in the brush where White Crow would not see him. When the people came along, they were to kill and butcher him, but they were to leave behind his skeleton and his head with the antlers attached.

So, the next morning, the people moved to where he had directed them and some of them went out to look for game. A hunter scared up the elk, chased him, and killed him. They butchered him the way they had been told.

While they had been chasing him, White Crow had flown over Elk and said, "I wonder how I overlooked you. I should have told you they were hunting and to hide. I am to blame. But you can run fast and save yourself."

After the hunters left: White Crow found the skeleton. He sat on its antlers and thought to himself, "I know this is not an elk, I know what Coyote did before. This is just Coyote, who has disguised himself again. I will test him and find out." So White Crow stood on Elk's head and began to strike at Elk's nose with his sharp beak saying, "I know you are Coyote! I know you are Coyote!" He kept on striking. He stopped just as Coyote was about to cry out. "Well, I will try another place." He moved back to the hind leg, to the kneecap. He struck with his beak. "I know you are Coyote! I know you are Coyote!" Again, Coyote was just about to yell when White Crow stopped.

"Well, you must be an elk, but I do not see how I overlooked you." White Crow than decided he would pick out the scraps of meat left on the ribs. When he stuck his head in between them, Coyote closed his ribs and held

White Crow in a vise. Then he got up and turned himself into a man. "Now, I have got you!"

White Crow said, "Coyote, please turn me loose. I will not do anything bad again. I will be good to you all. Please, turn me loose!"

The people were watching from a distance and when they saw that Coyote had White Crow, they began to shout.

Coyote said, "Now I have caught you and I am going to take you to camp and let the people do as they please with you." He took him to the camp and the people said, "This is the one who has caused us a lot of misery and starved us. Now that we have him, what shall we do with him?"

Spider Old Woman said, "Let me have him. I want to see the one who has caused us to starve." As she held White Crow, she was entangling him with her web but no one knew this. As she was doing it, White Crow got out of her hands and flew up into the air. He circled the camp, laughing. "This time I will have no compassion on you. This time I am really going to starve you!"

Coyote turned to Spider Old Woman and said, "I am going to tell the people to kill you for letting White Crow get away." Spider Old Woman said, "That White Crow doesn't know what he's talking about. I will get him." She began dragging in White Crow as though she was pulling on a rope. White Crow said. "Hey, I was only joking. I will be good. Have compassion on me." But Spider Old Woman went on pulling him in until she got him in her hands. She gave him to Coyote. "Do whatever you want with him," she said.

Coyote ordered the men to go and get firewood. They built a big fire and put White Crow in it until he was burned all black. Then Coyote said, "I am going to make it so you can never do anything your own way. All your life you are going to be a bird flying about looking for scraps. You are going to be frightened by everything."

Now, this is the way with Crow. (Kiowa)

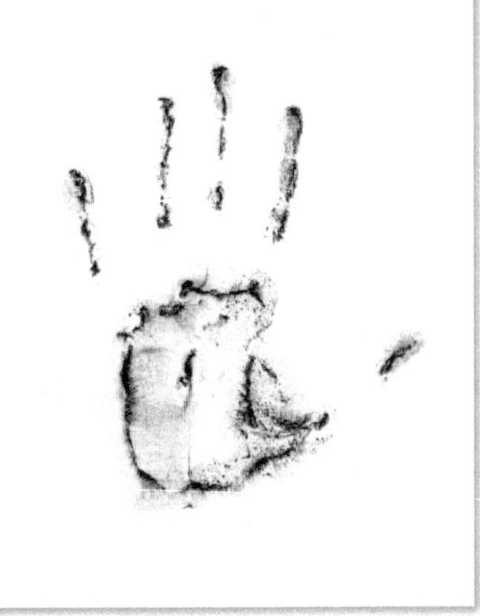

The Eye Juggler

*A Cheyenne Legend
Kroeber,. Journal of
American Folk-Lore,
xiii, 168, No. 11*

There was a man that could send his eyes out of his head, on the limb of a tree, and call them back again, by saying "Eyes hang upon a branch."

White-man saw him doing this, and came to him crying; he wanted to learn this too.

The man taught him, but warned him not to do it more than four times in one day. White-man went off along the river. When he came to the highest tree he could see, he sent his eyes to the top. Then he called them back. He thought he could do this as often as he wished, disregarding the warning.

The fifth time his eyes remained fastened to the limb. All day he called, but the eyes began to swell and spoil, and flies gathered on them. White-man grew tired and lay down, facing his eyes, still calling for them, though they never came; and he cried. At night he was half asleep, when a mouse ran over him. He closed his lids that the mice would not see he was blind, and lay still, in order to catch one.

At last, one sat on his breast. He kept quiet to let it become used to him, and the mouse went on his face, trying to cut his hair for its nest. Then it licked his tears, but let its tail hang in his mouth. He closed it, and caught the mouse. He seized it tightly, and made it guide him, telling him of his misfortune. The mouse said it could see the eyes, and they had swelled to an enormous size. It offered to climb the tree and get them for him, but White-man would not let it go. It tried to wriggle free, but he held it fast. Then the mouse asked on what condition he would release it, and White-man said, only if it gave him one of its eyes. So, it gave him one, and he could see again, and let the mouse go. But the small eye was far back in his socket, and he could not see very well with it.

A buffalo was grazing nearby, and as White-man stood near him crying, he looked on and wondered. White-man said: "Here is a buffalo, who has the power to help me in my trouble." So, the Buffalo asked him what he wanted. White-man told him he had lost his eye and needed one. The buffalo took out one of his and put it in White-man's head. Now White-man could see far again. But the eye did not fit the socket; most of it was outside. The other was far inside. Thus, he remained.

The Magic Windpipe

An Arikara Legend

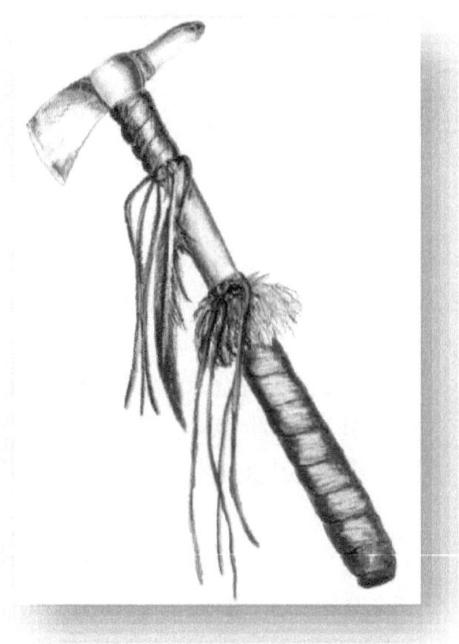

A long time ago there lived a beautiful Indian girl. Her lodge was on the edge of a forest, and she dwelt alone. And though she never hunted or fished, she always had plenty to eat, and no one knew where it came from. In her lodge hung a magic bundle, and near it were seven tiny bows and a lot of grass arrows.

One day as she was eating her dinner, Coyote came through the forest, and stopped at her door. He saw that she had roast Buffalo meat, and he licked his chops.

"You have no man around," said he to the girl; "may I stay and do your errands?"

"Yes," said she, "you may stay."

So, Coyote lived with her, and made her fires and brought water from the spring.

By and by all the Buffalo meat was gone, and Coyote wondered how she was going to get more. Then the girl said "Uncle Coyote, our food is gone. I want some fresh meat. My brothers will be here today. You go to the north side of the entrance and cover your head with a Buffalo robe, and don't watch what I do."

So, Coyote did as he was told, and when his head was covered, he peeped out and saw the girl sweep the lodge clean. Then she placed hot coals in the center of the room, and put some sweet-grass on the coals. As the smoke arose, she lifted the magic bundle from the wall, and opening it, took out the windpipe of a Buffalo. It was round, and small at one end, and big at the other.

She waved the windpipe over the smoke, and turned the small end down, and some dust fell out on the floor. Then the dust changed into seven handsome braves, her brothers.

The young men took down the tiny bows and arrows from the wall, and they changed into big bows and arrows.

The girl wrapped herself in a Buffalo robe, then went and stood in the door. She gave a yell to the north, and a yell to the west, and immediately herds of Buffalo came rushing over the plain. Then she went back into the lodge, and her brothers began to kill the Buffalo. When they had killed as many as they wanted, the rest of the animals ran away, and the brothers came back into the lodge.

The girl put more sweet-grass on the coals, and when the smoke rose up the brothers stepped behind it, and disappeared. The girl took the magic windpipe, held it over the coals, gathered up a handful of dust from the floor, and put it into the windpipe. After that she put the windpipe into the magic bundle and hung it again on the wall.

She next passed the big bows and arrows through the smoke and they became tiny bows and grass arrows, and she hung them up, too.

Now, Coyote was very much astonished to see all this, but he kept quiet. By and by the girl called him, and showed him the dead Buffalo. He helped her to skin the animals, and to dry the flesh. After that she let Coyote roast all the bones he wished.

When Coyote had eaten the roast meat, he began to think of his hungry children at home, and said to himself, "If I only had that magic windpipe, I could call the Buffalo whenever I wished, and the seven young braves would kill them for me."

Then he asked the girl if the windpipe held more than seven young men. "Oh, yes," said she; "whenever I turn the big end upside down, a war party comes out, headed by my seven brothers, and they fight for me."

When Coyote heard this, he decided to steal the windpipe that night, for he thought, "When my enemies see all those braves, they will think me powerful, and will run away."

Now the girl knew that Coyote was planning to steal the windpipe, and she let him take it. That night, when she was asleep, he lifted down the magic bundle from the wall, and, opening it, took out the windpipe and ran away fast toward the north.

He traveled far until he was tired, and then lay down by a log to sleep. The girl knew this, and she told her brothers to bring him back. They did so, and placed him on the floor of the lodge.

And when he woke in the morning, there he lay, with the magic windpipe in his paw, and the girl looking at him.

"Oh, my niece," said he, "I thought a war-party was coming in the night, so I took this down. Put it back." So, the girl tied the windpipe up in the magic bundle, and hung it on the wall.

The next night Coyote ran away again with the magic windpipe, and when he came to a place where he thought he was safe, he lay down to sleep. The girl told her brothers to bring him back. They did so, and placed him on the floor of the lodge.

And when he woke in the morning, there he lay, with the magic windpipe in his paw, and the girl looking at him.

"Oh, my niece," said he, "I took this down because the enemy came in the night, and I frightened him away. Put it back." So, the girl tied the windpipe up again, and hung it on the wall. And the same thing happened the third night.

The fourth time Coyote stole the magic windpipe, the girl let him take it and did not tell her brothers to bring him back. No, indeed! She let him go on until he came to a village. He was very hungry, so he said to himself, "I will call out the people and order them to feed me, and if they do not obey, I will turn the big end of the windpipe upside down, and the war-party will come out."

So, he called out the people, and the braves came running and shouting from the lodges, and the boys and dogs came too. And when they saw Coyote, the men and boys began to kick him, and throw stones at him, and the dogs bit him. He turned the windpipe upside down, when, instead of a war-party, outburst a whole swarm of Bumblebees, millions of them, buzzing with rage.

They settled all over Coyote, and stung him so hard that he ran howling into the forest. And they kept on stinging him until he was well punished for his lying and stealing.

After that, the Bumblebees swarmed up into a hollow tree, and they have lived there ever since. As for the magic windpipe, the brothers took it back to the girl.

The Fox and the Kingfisher

A Jicarilla Apache
Legend
Frank Russell, Myths of the Jicarilla Apaches, 1898

As Fox went on his way he met Kingfisher, Kêt-la'-i-le-ti, whom he accompanied to his home. Kingfisher said that he had no food to offer his visitor, so he would go and catch some fish for Fox. He broke through six inches of ice on the river and caught two fish, which he cooked and set before his guest.

Fox was pleased with his entertainment, and invited the Kingfisher to return the call. In due time the Kingfisher came to the home of the Fox, who said, "I have no food to offer you;" then he went down to the river, thinking to secure fish in the same manner as the Kingfisher had done.

Fox leaped from the high bank, but instead of breaking through the ice he broke his head and killed himself.

Kingfisher went to him, caught him up by the tail, and swung Fox around to the right four times, thereby restoring him to life. Kingfisher caught some fish, and they ate together.

"I am a medicine-man," said Kingfisher; "that is why I can do these things. You must never try to catch fish in that way again."

After the departure of Kingfisher, Fox paid a visit to the home of Prairie-dog, where he was cordially received.

Prairie-dog put four sticks, each about a foot in length, in the ashes of the camp-fire; when these were removed, they proved to be four nicely roasted prairie-dogs, which were served for Fox's dinner.

Fox invited the Prairie-dog to return the visit, which in a short time the latter did. Fox placed four sticks in the fire to roast, but they were consumed by it, and instead of palatable food to set before his guest he had nothing but ashes. Prairie-dog said to Fox, "You must not attempt to do that. I am a medicine-man; that is why I can transform the wood to flesh." Prairie-dog then prepared a meal as he done before, and they dined.

Fox went to visit Buffalo, I-gûn-da, who exclaimed, "What shall I do? I have no food to offer you. Buffalo was equal to the emergency, however; he shot an arrow upward, which struck in his own back as it returned. When he pulled this out, a kidney and the fat surrounding it came out also. This he cooked for Fox, and added a choice morsel from his own nose.

As usual, Fox extended an invitation to his host to return the visit. When Buffalo came to call upon Fox, the latter covered his head with weeds in imitation of the head of the Buffalo. Fox thought he could provide food for their dinner as the Buffalo had done, so fired an arrow into the air; but when it came close to him on its return flight, he became frightened and ran away.

Buffalo then furnished meat for their meal as on the previous occasion. "You must not try this," said he; "I am a medicine-man; that is why I have the power."

Some time afterward, as Fox was journeying along, he met an Elk, Tsês, lying beside the trail. He was frightened when he saw the antlers of the Elk moving, and jumped to avoid what seemed to be a falling tree.

"Sit down beside me," said the Elk. "Don't be afraid."

"The tree will fall on us," replied Fox.

"Oh, sit down; it won't fall. I have no food to offer you, but I will provide some." The Elk cut steaks from his own quarter, which the Fox ate, and before leaving Fox invited the Elk to return the visit.

When Elk came to see Fox, the latter tried unsuccessfully to cut flesh from his own meager flanks; then he drove sharpened sticks into his nose, and allowed the blood to run out upon the grass. This he tried in vain to transform into meat, and again he was indebted to his guest for a meal.

"I am a medicine-man; that is why I can do this," said Elk.

Story Of the Peace Pipe

*Myths and Legends of the Sioux McLaughlin, Marie L.
(1916)*

Two young men were out strolling one night talking of love
affairs. They passed around a hill and came to a little ravine
or coulee. Suddenly they saw coming up from the ravine a
beautiful woman. She was painted and her dress was of the
very finest material.

"What a beautiful girl!" said one of the young men.
"Already I love her. I will steal her and make her my wife."

"No," said the other. "Don't harm her. She may be holy."

The young woman approached and held out a pipe which
she first offered to the sky, then to the earth and then
advanced, holding it out in her extended hands.

"I know what you young men have been saying; one of you
is good; the other is wicked," she said.

She laid down the pipe on the ground and at once became a
buffalo cow. The cow pawed the ground, stuck her tail

straight out behind her and then lifted the pipe from the ground again in her hoofs; immediately she became a young woman again.

"I am come to give you this gift," she said. "It is the peace pipe. Hereafter all treaties and ceremonies shall be performed after smoking it. It shall bring peaceful thoughts into your minds. You shall offer it to the Great Mystery and to mother earth."

The two young men ran to the village and told what they had seen and heard. All the village came out where the young woman was.

She repeated to them what she had already told the young men and added:

"When you set free the ghost (the spirit of deceased persons) you must have a white buffalo cow skin."

She gave the pipe to the medicine men of the village, turned again to a buffalo cow and fled away to the land of buffaloes.

Dance in a Buffalo Skull

It was night upon the prairie. Overhead the stars were twinkling bright their red and yellow lights. The moon was young. A silvery thread among the stars, it soon drifted low beneath the horizon.

Upon the ground the land was pitchy black. There are night people on the plain who love the dark. Amid the black level land, they meet to frolic under the stars. Then when their sharp ears hear any strange footfalls nigh, they scamper away into the deep shadows of night. There they are safely hid from all dangers; they think.

Thus, it was that one very black night, afar off from the edge of the level land, out of the wooded river bottom glided forth two balls of fire. They came farther and farther into the level land. They grew larger and brighter. The dark hid the body of the creature with those fiery eyes. They came on and on, just over the tops of the prairie grass. It might have been a wildcat prowling low on soft, stealthy feet. Slowly but surely the terrible eyes drew nearer and nearer to the heart of the level land.

There in a huge old buffalo skull was a gay feast and dance! Tiny little field mice were singing and dancing in a circle to the boom-boom of a wee, wee drum. They were laughing and talking among themselves while their chosen singers sang loud a merry tune.

They built a small open fire within the center of their queer dance house. The light streamed out of the buffalo skull through all the curious sockets and holes.

A light on the plain in the middle of the night was an unusual thing. But so merry were the mice they did not hear the "king, king" of sleepy birds, disturbed by the unaccustomed fire.

A pack of wolves, fearing to come nigh this night fire, stood together a little distance away, and, turning their pointed noses to the stars, howled and yelped most dismally. Even the cry of the wolves was unheeded by the mice within the lighted buffalo skull.

They were feasting and dancing; they were singing and laughing -- those funny little furry fellows.

All the while across the dark from out the low river bottom came that pair of fiery eyes.

Now closer and more swift, now fiercer and glaring, the eyes moved toward the buffalo skull. All unconscious of those fearful eyes, the happy mice nibbled dried roots and venison. The singers had started another song. The drummers beat the time, turning their heads from side to side in rhythm. In a ring around the fire hopped the mice, each bouncing hard on his two hind feet. Some carried their tails over their arms, while others trailed them proudly along.

Ah, very near are those round yellow eyes! Very low to the ground they seem to creep -- creep toward the buffalo skull. All of a sudden, they slide into the eye- sockets of the old skull.

"Spirit of the buffalo!" squeaked a frightened mouse as he jumped out from a hole in the back part of the skull.

"A cat! a cat!" cried other mice as they scrambled out of holes both large and snug. Noiseless they ran away into the dark.

Tale of the Girl Who Had Power to Call the Buffalo

Dorsey, George A. Traditions of the Caddo. Washington: Carnegie Institution. 1905.

A girl who had power to call the buffalo lived with her six brothers. The brothers were stars, and every night they left the girl to travel through the sky. Every morning after they had returned from their nightly journey, they put the girl in a swing of lariat rope that hung down from the sky and swung her through the air. As she swung through the air the buffalo saw her and came. The boys killed all that they wanted, and then the rest of the herd went away. In this way the girl called the buffalo for her brothers, and so they always had plenty to eat.

One time Coyote came to visit them, and, finding that they always had meat, he decided to come and live with them. The brothers did not think much of Coyote, but they decided to let him stay. Every morning he watched the boys put their sister in the swing and swing her until the buffalo came. Before the brothers would let Coyote watch them swing her, they made him promise that he would never try to do the same while they were gone, because if any one else tried to swing the girl, he would swing her too hard and she would swing to the sky and never return. Coyote promised, but one day while all of the brothers were gone, he called the girl to come and get into the swing. She refused, but he threatened her and made her obey him. She climbed into the swing and Coyote pushed her. The buffalo did not come, and so he pushed her again and caused her to go higher and higher through the air until she disappeared. Coyote became frightened and called to her to come down, saying that if she did not come, he would jump up and pull her down. The girl did not come, and he could not see her.

When the brothers came home, they missed their sister and asked Coyote where she was. He said that he did not know, but that he thought some monster had carried her away. The brothers knew that Coyote had lied, and that he had been the cause of her disappearance. They drove Coyote away, telling him that he and his children would always be hungry because he had disobeyed them. Then they held a council among themselves and decided to go to the sky and live there with their sister.

Falling-Star
A Cheyenne Legend

One day in the long ago, two young Indian girls were lying on the grass outside their tepee on a warm summer evening. They were looking up into the sky, describing star-pictures formed by their imaginations.

"That is a pretty star. I like that one," said First Girl.

"I like that one best of all--over there," Second Girl pointed.

First Girl pointed to the brightest star in the sky and said, "I like the brightest one best of all. That is the one I want to marry."

That evening they agreed to go out the next day to gather wood. Next morning, they started for the timbered area. On their way they saw a porcupine climb a tree.

"I'll climb the tree and pull him down," said First Girl. She climbed but could not reach the porcupine.

Every time she stretched her hand for him, the porcupine climbed a little higher. Then the tree started growing taller. Second Girl below called to her friend, "Please come down, the tree is growing taller!"

"No," said First Girl as the porcupine climbed higher and the tree grew taller. Second Girl could see what was happening, so she ran back to the camp and told her people. They rushed to the tree, but First Girl had completely disappeared!

The tree continued to grow higher and higher. Finally, First Girl reached another land. She stepped off the tree branch and walked upon the sky! Before long she met a kindly looking middle-aged man who spoke to her. First Girl began to cry.

"Whatever is the matter? Only last night I heard you wish that you could marry me. I am the Brightest-Star," he said.

First Girl was pleased to meet Brightest-Star and became happy again when she got her wish and married him. He told her that she could dig roots with the other star-women, but to beware of a certain kind of white turnip with a great green top. This kind she must never dig. To do so was "against the medicine"--against the rules of the Sky-Chief.

Every day First Girl dug roots. Her curiosity about the strange white turnip became so intense that she decided to dig up one of them. It took her a long, long time. When she finally pulled out the root, a huge hole was left. She looked into the hole and far, far below she saw the camp of her own people.

Everything and everyone was very small, but she could see lodges and people walking. Instantly she became homesick to see her own people again. How could she ever get down from the sky? She realized it was a long, long way down to earth. Then her eyes fell upon the long tough grass growing near her. Could she braid it into a long rope? She decided to try, every day pulling more long grass and braiding more rope.

One time her husband Brightest-Star asked, "What is it that keeps you outdoors so much of the time?"

"I walk a great distance and that makes me tired. I need to sit down and rest before I can start back home."

At last, she finished making her strong rope, thinking by now it must be long enough. She tied one end of the rope to a log that she rolled across the top of the hole as an anchor. She let down the rope. It looked as though it touched the ground.

She lowered herself into the hole, holding onto the braided rope. It seemed to take a long time as she slowly lowered herself until she came to the end of the rope. But it did not touch the earth! For a long while she hung on dangling in midair and calling uselessly for help. When she could hold on no longer, she fell to the ground and broke into many pieces. Although she died, her unborn son did not die, because he was made of star-stone and did not break.

A meadowlark saw what happened and took the falling-star baby to her nest. There the lark kept him with her own baby birds. When they were older, Falling-Star crept out of the nest with the little birds. The stronger the birds grew, the stronger grew Falling-Star. Soon all of them could crawl and run. The young birds practiced their flying while Falling-Star ran after them. Then the young birds could fly anywhere they wished, while Falling-Star ran faster and faster to keep up with them.

"Son, you had better go home to your own people," said Mother Meadowlark. "It is time for us to fly south for the winter. Before long, the weather here will be very cold."

"Mother Meadowlark," asked Falling-Star. "Why do you want me to leave you? I want to go with you."

"No, Son," she replied. "You must go home now."

"I will go if Father Meadowlark will make me a bow and some arrows."

Father Meadowlark made a bow and pulled some of his own quills to feather the arrows. He made four arrows and a bow for Falling- Star. Then he started Falling-Star in the right direction toward his home, downstream.

Falling-Star travelled a long time before he reached the camp of his people. He went into the nearest lodge owned by an old grandmother.

"Grandmother," he said. "I need a drink of water."

"My grandson," she said to him, "only the young men who are the fastest runners can go for water. There is a water-monster who sucks up any people who go too close to it."

"Grandmother, if you will give me your buffalo-pouch and your buffalo-horn ladle, I will bring you water."

"Grandson, I warn you that many of our finest young men have been destroyed by the water-monster. I fear that you will be killed, too." But she gave him the things he asked for. He went upstream and dipped water, at the same time keeping watch for the monster.

At the very moment Falling-Star filled his bucket, the Water-monster raised its head above the water. His mouth was enormous. He sucked in his breath and drew in Falling-Star, the bucket, water, and the ladle. When Falling-Star found himself inside the monster's stomach, he saw all the other people who had ever been swallowed. With his Star-stone, he cut a hole in the animal's side. Out crawled all the people and Falling-Star rescued his pouch and ladle for his grandmother, taking her some cool, fresh water.

"My grandson, who are you?" she asked, marveling at his survival.

"Grandmother, I am Falling-Star. I killed the monster that has caused our people much suffering, and I rescued all the people who had been swallowed."

The old woman told the village crier to spread the good news that the monster was dead. Now that Falling-Star had saved the camp people there, he asked the grandmother, "Are there other camps of our people nearby?"

"Yes, there is one farther downstream," she said.

Falling-Star took his bow and arrows and left camp. The fall of the year had now arrived. After travelling many days, he reached the other camp. Again, he went into an old woman's lodge where she sat near her fire.

"Grandmother, I am very hungry," he said.

"My son, my son, we have no food. We cannot get any buffalo meat. Whenever our hunters go out for buffalo, a great white crow warns the buffalo, which drives them away.

"How sad," he said. "I will try to help. Go out and look for a worn-out buffalo robe with little hair. Tell your chief to choose two of his fastest runners and send them to me."

Later, the old woman returned with the robe and the two swift runners. Falling-Star told them his plan. "I will go to a certain place and wait for the buffalo. When the herd runs, I will follow, disguised as a buffalo in the worn-out robe. You two runners chase me and the buffalo for a long distance. When you overtake me, you must shoot at me. I will pretend to be dead. You pretend to cut me open and leave me there on the ground."

When the real buffalo arrived, the white crow flew over them screaming, "They are coming! They are after you! Run, run!" The buffalo herd ran, followed by a shabby-looking bull.

The two swift runners chased the old bull according to plan. All kinds of birds, wolves, and coyotes came toward the carcass from all directions. Among them was the white crow. As he flew over Falling-Star in disguise, he called out shrilly, "I wonder if this is Falling-Star?"

Time after time the crow flew over the carcass, still calling, "I wonder if this is Falling-Star?" He came closer and closer with each pass. When he was close enough, Falling-Star sprang and grabbed the legs of the white crow. All of the other birds and animals scattered in every direction.

When Falling-Star brought the captive white crow home to the grandmother, she sent word for the chief.

"I will take the white crow to my lodge. I will tie him to the smoke hole and smoke him dead," said the chief.

From that moment on, the good Cheyenne were able to kill many buffalo and they had plenty of buffalo meat for all their needs.

The people in gratitude gave Falling-Star a lovely lodge-home and a pretty Indian maiden waiting there to become his wife. They remained all of their lives with the Northern Cheyenne Indian tribe.

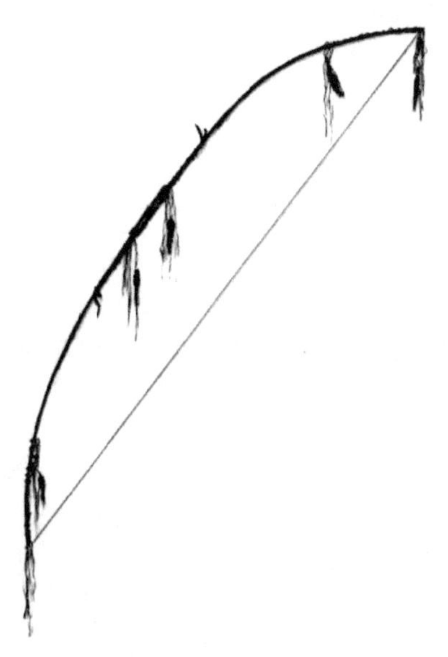

Blood Clot Boy

A Blackfoot Legend

Once there was an old
man and woman
whose three daughters
married a young man.
The old people lived
in a lodge by
themselves.

The young man was
supposed to hunt
buffalo, and feed them
all. Early in the
morning the young
man invited his father-in-law to go out with him to kill
buffalo. The old man was then directed to drive the buffalo
through a gap where the young man stationed himself to
kill them as they went by. As soon as the buffalo were
killed, the young man requested his father-in-law to go
home.

He said, "You are old. You need not stay here. Your
daughters can bring you some meat." Now the young man
lied to his father-in-law; for when the meat was brought to
his lodge, he ordered his wives not to give meat to the old
folks. Yet one of the daughters took pity on her parents,
and stole meat for them. The way in which she did this was
to take a piece of meat in her robe, and as she went for
water drop it in front of her father's lodge.

Now every morning the young man invited his father-in-
law to hunt buffalo; and, as before, sent him away and

refused to permit his daughters to furnish meat for the old people. On the fourth day, as the old man was returning, he saw a clot of blood in the trail, and said to himself, "Here at least is something from which we can make soup."

In order that he might not be seen by his son-in-law, he stumbled, and spilt the arrows out of his quiver. Now, as he picked up the arrows, he put the clot of blood into the quiver. Just then the young man came up and demanded to know what it was he picked up. The old man explained that he had just stumbled, and was picking up his arrows.

So, the old man took the clot of blood home and requested his wife to make blood-soup. When the pot began to boil, the old woman heard a child crying. She looked all around, but saw nothing. Then she heard it again. This time it seemed to be in the pot. She looked in quickly, and saw a boy baby: so, she lifted the pot from the fire, took the baby out and wrapped it up.

Now the young man, sitting in his lodge, heard a baby crying, and said, "Well, the old woman must have a baby." Then he sent his oldest wife over to see the old woman's baby, saying, "If it is a boy, I will kill it." The woman came into look at the baby, but the old woman told her it was a girl. When the young man heard this, he did not believe it.

So, he sent each wife in turn; but they all came back with the same report. Now the young man was greatly pleased, because he could look forward to another wife. So, he sent over some old bones, that soup might be made for the baby. Now, all this happened in the morning.

That night the baby spoke to the old man, saying, "You take me up and hold me against each lodge-pole in succession." So, the old man took up the baby, and, beginning at the door, went around in the direction of the sun, and each time that he touched a pole the baby became larger. When halfway around, the baby was so heavy that the old man could hold him no longer. So, he put the baby down in the middle of the lodge, and, taking hold of his head, moved it toward each of the poles in succession, and, when the last pole was reached, the baby had become a very fine young man.

Then this young man went out, got some black flint [obsidian] and, when he got to the lodge, he said to the old man, "I am the Smoking-Star. I came down to help you. When I have done this, I shall return."

Now, when morning came, Blood-Clot (the name his father gave him) arose and took his father out to hunt. They had not gone very far when they killed a scabby cow. Then Blood-Clot lay down behind the cow and requested his father to wait until the son-in-law came to join him. He also requested that he stand his ground and talk back to the son-in-law.

Now, at the usual time in the morning, the son-in-law called at the lodge of the old man, but was told that he had gone out to hunt. This made him very angry, and he struck at the old woman, saying, "I have a notion to kill you." So, the son-in-law went out.

Now Blood-Clot had directed his father to be eating a kidney when the son-in- law approached. When the son-in-law came up and saw all this, he was very angry. He said to the old man, "Now you shall die for all this."

"Well," said the old man, "you must die too, for all that you have done."

Then the son in-law began to shoot arrows at the old man, and the latter becoming frightened called on Blood-Clot for help. Then Blood-Clot sprang up and upbraided the son-in-law for his cruelty. "Oh," said the son-in-law, "I was just fooling." At this Blood-Clot shot the son-in-law through and through.

Then Blood-Clot said to his father, "We will leave this meat here: it is not good. Your son-in-law's house is full of dried meat. Which one of your daughters helped you?"

The old man told him that it was the youngest.

Then Blood-Clot went to the lodge, killed the two older women, brought up the body of the son-in-law, and burned them together. Then he requested the younger daughter to take care of her old parents, to be kind to them, etc. "Now," said Blood-Clot, "I shall go to visit the other Indians."

So, he started out, and finally came to a camp. He went into the lodge of some old women, who were very much surprised to see such a fine young man. They said, "Why do you come here among such old women as we? Why don't you go where there are young people?"

"Well," said Blood-Clot, "give me some dried meat." Then the old women gave him some meat, but no fat. "Well," said Blood-Clot, "you did not give me the fat to eat with my dried meat."

"Hush!" said the old women. "You must not speak so loud. There are bears here that take all the fat and give us the lean, and they will kill you, if they hear you."

"Well," said Blood-Clot, "I will go out to-morrow, do some butchering, and get some fat." Then he went out through the camp, telling all the people to make ready in the morning, for he intended to drive the buffalo over [the drive].

Now there were some bears who ruled over this camp. They lived in a bear- lodge [painted lodge], and were very cruel. When Blood-Clot had driven the buffalo over, he noticed among them a scabby cow. He said, "I shall save this for the old women."

Then the people laughed, and said, "Do you mean to save that poor old beast? It is too poor to have fat." However, when it was cut open it was found to be very fat. Now, when the bears heard the buffalo go over the drive, they as usual sent out two bears to cut off the best meat, especially all the fat; but Blood-Clot had already butchered the buffalo, putting the fat upon sticks. He hid it as the bears came up.

Also, he had heated some stones in a fire. When they told him what they wanted, he ordered them to go back. Now the bears were very angry, and the chief bear and his wife came up to fight, but Blood-Clot killed them by throwing hot stones down their throats.

Then he went down to the lodge of the bears and killed all, except one female who was about to become a mother. She pleaded so pitifully for her life, that he spared her. If he had not done this, there would have been no more bears in the world.

The lodge of the bears was filled with dried meat and other property. Also, all the young women of the camp were confined there. Blood-Clot gave all the property to the old women, and set free all the young women. The bears' lodge he gave to the old women. It was a bear painted lodge.

"Now," said Blood-Clot, "I must go on my travels."

He came to a camp and entered the lodge of some old women. When these women saw what a fine young man he was, they said, "Why do you come here, among such old women? Why do you not go where there are younger people?"

"Well," said he, "give me some meat." The old women gave him some dried meat, but no fat.

Then he said, "Why do you not give me some fat with my meat?"

"Hush!" said the women, "you must not speak so loud. There is a snake- lodge [painted lodge] here, and the snakes take everything. They leave no fat for the people."

"Well," said Blood-Clot, "I will go over to the snake-lodge to eat."

"No, you must not do that," said the old women. "It is dangerous. They will surely kill you."

"Well," said he, "I must have some fat with my meat, even if they do kill me."

Then he entered the snake-lodge. He had his white rock knife ready. Now the snake, who was the head man in this lodge, had one horn on his head. He was lying with his head in the lap of a beautiful woman. He was asleep. By the fire was a bowl of berry-soup ready for the snake when he should wake. Blood-Clot seized the bowl and drank the soup.

Then the women warned him in whispers, "You must go away: you must not stay here." But he said, "I want to smoke." So, he took out his knife and cut off the head of the snake, saying as he did so, "Wake up! light a pipe! I want to smoke."

Then with his knife he began to kill all the snakes. At last, there was one snake who was about to become a mother, and she pleaded so pitifully for her life that she was allowed to go. From her descended all the snakes that are in the world.

Now the lodge of the snakes was filled up with dried meat of every kind, fat, etc. Blood-Clot turned all this over to the people, the lodge and everything it contained. Then he said, "I must go away and visit other people."

So, he started out. Some old women advised him to keep on the south side of the road, because it was dangerous the other way. But Blood-Clot paid no attention to their warning. As he was going along, a great windstorm struck him and at last carried him into the mouth of a great fish.

This was a sucker-fish and the wind was its sucking. When he got into the stomach of the fish, he saw a great many people. Many of them were dead, but some were still alive. He said to the people, "Ah, there must be a heart somewhere here. We will have a dance."

So, he painted his face white, his eyes and mouth with black circles, and tied a white rock knife on his head, so that the point stuck up. Some rattles made of hoofs were also brought. Then the people started in to dance. For a while Blood-Clot sat making wing-motions with his hands, and singing songs. Then he stood up and danced, jumping up and down until the knife on his head struck the heart.

Then he cut the heart down. Next, he cut through between the ribs of the fish, and let all the people out.

Again Blood-Clot said he must go on his travels. Before starting, the people warned him, saying that after a while he would see a woman who was always challenging people to wrestle with her, but that he must not speak to her. He gave no heed to what they said, and, after he had gone a little way, he saw a woman who called him to come over. "No," said Blood-Clot. "I am in a hurry."

However, at the fourth time the woman asked him to come over, he said, "Yes, but you must wait a little while, for I am tired. I wish to rest. When I have rested, I will come over and wrestle with you."

Now, while he was resting, he saw many large knives sticking up from the ground almost hidden by straw. Then he knew that the woman killed the people she wrestled with by throwing them down on the knives. When he was rested, he went over.

The woman asked him to stand up in the place where he had seen the knives; but he said, "No, I am not quite ready. Let us play a little, before we begin." So, he began to play with the woman, but quickly caught hold of her, threw her upon the knives, and cut her in two.

Blood-Clot took up his travels again, and after a while came to a camp where there were some old women. The old women told him that a little farther on he would come to a woman with a swing, but on no account must he ride with her.

After a time, he came to a place where he saw a swing on the bank of a swift stream. There was a woman swinging on it. He watched her a while, and saw that she killed people by swinging them out and dropping them into the water. When he found this out, he came up to the woman. "You have a swing here; let me see you swing," he said.

"No," said the woman, "I want to see you swing."

"Well," said Blood-Clot, "but you must swing first"

"Well,'" said the woman, "Now I shall swing. Watch me. Then I shall see you do it." So, the woman swung out over the stream. As she did this, he saw how it worked. Then he said to the woman, "You swing again while I am getting ready"; but as the woman swung out this time, he cut the vine and let her drop into the water.

This happened on Cut Bank Creek.

"Now," said Blood-Clot, "I have rid the world of all the monsters, I will go back to my old father and mother." So, he climbed a high ridge, and returned to the lodge of the old couple.

One day he said to them, "I shall go back to the place from whence I came. If you find that I have been killed, you must not be sorry, for then I shall go up into the sky and become the Smoking-Star."

Then he went on and on, until he was killed by some Crow Indians on the war- path. His body was never found; but the moment he was killed, the Smoking- Star appeared in the sky, where we see it now.

Buffalo Woman, a Story of Magic
Caddo

Snow Bird, the Caddo medicine man, had a handsome son. When the boy was old enough to be given a man's name, Snow Bird called him Braveness because of his courage as a hunter. Many of the girls in the Caddo village wanted to win Braveness as a husband, but he paid little attention to any of them.

One morning he started out for a day of hunting, and while he was walking along looking for wild game, he saw someone ahead of him sitting under a small elm tree. As he approached, he was surprised to find that the person was a young woman, and he started to turn aside.

"Come here," she called to him in a pleasant voice. Braveness went up to her and saw that she was very young and very beautiful.

"I knew you were coming here," she said, "and so I came to meet you."

"You are not of my people," he replied. "How did you know that I was coming this way?"

"I am Buffalo Woman," she said. "I have seen you many times before, from afar. I want you to take me home with you and let me stay with you."

"I can take you home with me," Braveness answered her, "but you must ask my parents if you can stay with us."

They started for his home at once, and when they arrived their Buffalo Woman asked Braveness's parents if she could stay with them and become the young man's wife. "If Braveness wants you for his wife, we will be pleased," said Snow Bird, the medicine man. "It is time that he had someone to love."

And so, Braveness and Buffalo Woman were married in the custom of the Caddo people and lived happily together for several moons. One day she asked him, "Will you do whatever I may ask of you, Braveness?"

"Yes," he replied, "if what you ask is not unreasonable."

"I want you to go with me to visit my people."

Braveness said that he would go, and the next day they started for her home, she leading the way. After they had walked a long distance they came to some high hills, and all at once she turned round and looked at Braveness and said: "You promised me that you would do anything I say." "Yes," he answered.

"Well," she said, "my home is on the other side of this high hill. I will tell you when we get to my mother. I know there will be many coming there to see who you are, and some may provoke you and try to make you angry, but do not allow yourself to become angry with any of them. Some may try to kill you."

"Why should they do that?" asked Braveness.

"Listen to what I am about to tell you," She said. "I knew you before you knew me. Through magic I made you come to me that first day. I said that some will try to make you angry, and if you show anger at even one of them, the others will join in fighting you until they have killed you. They will be jealous of you. The reason is that I refused many who wanted me."

"But you are now my wife," Braveness said.

"I have told you what to do when we get there," Buffalo Woman continued. "Now I want you to lie down on the ground and roll over twice."

Braveness smiled at her, but he did as she had told him to do. He rolled over twice, and when he stood up, he found himself changed into a Buffalo.

For a moment Buffalo Woman looked at him, seeing the astonishment in his eyes. Then she rolled over twice, and she also became a Buffalo. Without saying a word, she led him to the top of the hill. In the valley off to the west, Braveness could see hundreds and hundreds of Buffalo.

"They are my people," said Buffalo Woman. "This is my home."

When the members of the nearest herd saw Braveness and Buffalo Woman coming, they began gathering in one place, as though waiting for them. Buffalo Woman led the way, Braveness following her until they reached an old Buffalo cow, and he knew that she was the mother of his beautiful wife.

For two moons they stayed with the herd. Every now and then, four or five of the young Buffalo males would come around and annoy Braveness, trying to arouse his anger, but he pretended not to notice them. One night, Buffalo Woman told him that she was ready to go back to his home, and they slipped away over the hills.

When they reached the place where they had turned themselves into Buffalo, they rolled over twice on the ground and became a man and a woman again. "Promise me that you will not tell anyone of this magical transformation," Buffalo Woman said. "If people learn about it, something bad will happen to us."

They stayed at Braveness's home for twelve moons, and then Buffalo Woman asked him again to go with her to visit her people. They had not been long in the valley of the Buffalo when she told Braveness that the young males who were jealous of him were planning to have a foot-race.

"They will challenge you to race and if you do not outrun them, they will kill you," she said.

That night Braveness could not sleep. He went out to take a long walk. It was a very dark night without moon or stars, but he could feel the presence of the Wind spirit.

"You are young and strong," the Wind spirit whispered to him, "but you cannot outrun the Buffalo without my help. If you lose, they will kill you. If you win, they will never challenge you again.

"What must I do to save my life and keep my beautiful wife?" asked Braveness.

The Wind spirit gave him two things. "One of these is a magic herb," said the Wind spirit. "The other is dried mud from a medicine wallow. If the Buffalo catch up with you, first throw behind you the magic herb. If they come too close to you again, throw down the dried mud."

The next day was the day of the race. At sunrise the young Buffalo gathered at the starting place. When Braveness joined them, they began making fun of him, telling him he was a man buffalo and therefore had not the power to outrun them. Braveness ignored their jeers, and calmly lined up with them at the starting point.

An old Buffalo started the race with a loud bellow, and at first Braveness took the lead, running very swiftly. But soon the others began gaining on him, and when he heard their hard breathing close upon his heels, he threw the magic herb behind him. By this time, he was growing very tired and thought he could not run any more. He looked back and saw one Buffalo holding his head down and coming very fast, rapidly closing the space between him and Braveness. Just as this Buffalo was about to catch up with him, Braveness threw down the dried mud from the medicine wallow.

Soon he was far ahead again, but he knew that he had used up the powers given him by the Wind spirit. As he neared the goal set for the race, he heard the pounding of hooves coming closer behind him. At the last moment, he felt a strong wind on his face as it passed him to stir up dust and keep the Buffalo from overtaking him. With the help of the Wind spirit, Braveness crossed the goal first and won the race. After that, none of the Buffalo ever challenged him again, and he and Buffalo Woman lived peacefully with the herd until they were ready to return to his Caddo people.

Not long after their return to Braveness's home, Buffalo Woman gave birth to a handsome son.

They named him Buffalo Boy, and soon he was old enough to play with the other children of the village. One day while Buffalo Woman was cooking dinner, the boy slipped out of the lodge and went to join some other children at play. They played several games and then decided to play that they were Buffalo. Some of them lay on the ground to roll like Buffalo, and Buffalo Boy also did this. When he rolled over twice, he changed into a real Buffalo calf. Frightened by this, the other children ran for their lodges.

About this time his mother came out to look for him, and when she saw the children running in fear, she knew that something must be wrong. She went to see what had happened and found her son changed into a Buffalo calf. Taking him up in her arms, she ran down the hill, and as soon as she was out of sight of the village, she turned herself into a Buffalo and with Buffalo Boy started off toward the west.

Late that evening when Braveness returned from hunting, he could find neither his wife nor his son in the lodge. He went out to look for them, and someone told him of the game the children had played and of the magic that had changed his son into a Buffalo calf.

At first, Braveness could not believe what they told him, but after he had followed his wife's tracks down the hill and found the place where she had rolled, he knew the story was true. For many moons, Braveness searched for Buffalo Woman and Buffalo Boy, but he never found them again.

How the Crow Came to be Black

A Brule Sioux Legend
- *Told by Good White Buffalo at Winner, Rosebud Indian Reservation, South Dakota, 1964.*

In days long past, when the earth and the people on it were still young, all crows were white as snow. In those ancient times the people had neither horses nor firearms nor weapons of iron. Yet they depended upon the buffalo hunt to give them enough food to survive.

Hunting the big buffalo on foot with stone-tipped weapons was hard, uncertain, and dangerous. The crows made things even more difficult for the hunters, because they were friends of the buffalo. Soaring high above the prairie, they could see everything that was going on. Whenever they spied hunters approaching a buffalo herd, they flew to their friends and, perching between their horns, warned them: "Caw, caw, caw, cousins, hunters are coming. They are creeping up through that gully over there. They are coming up behind that hill. Watch out! Caw, caw, caw!" Hearing this, the buffalo would stampede, and the people starved.

The people held a council to decide what to do. Now, among the crows was a huge one, twice as big as all the others. This crow was their leader. One wise old chief got up and made this suggestion: "We must capture the big white crow," he said, "and teach him a lesson. It's either that or go hungry."

He brought out a large buffalo skin, with the head and horns still attached. He put it on the back of a young brave, saying: "Nephew, sneak among the buffalo. They will think you are one of them, and you can capture the big white crow."

Disguised as a buffalo, the young man crept among the herd as if he were grazing. The big, shaggy beasts paid him no attention.

Then the hunters marched out from their camp after him, their bows at the ready. As they approached the herd, the crows came flying, as usual, warning the buffalo: "Caw, caw, caw, cousins, the hunters are coming to kill you. Watch out for their arrows. Caw, caw, caw!" and as usual, all the buffalo stampeded off and away - all, that is, except the young hunter in disguise under his shaggy skin, who pretended to go on grazing as before.

Then the big white crow came gliding down, perched on the hunter's shoulders, and flapping his wings, said: "Caw, caw, caw, brother, are you deaf? The hunters are close by, just over the hill. Save yourself!"

But the young brave reached out from under the buffalo skin and grabbed the crow by the legs.

With a rawhide string he tied the big bird's feet and fastened the other end to a stone. No matter how the crow struggled, he could not escape.

Again, the people sat in council. "What shall we do with this big, bad crow, who has made us go hungry again and again?"

"I'll burn him up!" answered one angry hunter, and before anybody could stop him, he yanked the crow from the hands of his captor and thrust it into the council fire, string, stone and all. "This will teach you," he said.

Of course, the string that held the stone burned through almost at once, and the big crow managed to fly out of the fire. But he was badly singed, and some of his feathers were charred. Though he was still big, he was no longer white.

"Caw, caw, caw," he cried, flying away as quickly as he could, "I'll never do it again; I'll stop warning the buffalo, and so will the Crow nation. I promise! Caw, caw, caw."

Thus, the crow escaped. But ever since, all crows have been black.

The Dog and The Stick

(Blackfoot Lodge Tales, George Bird Grinnell, 1892)

This happened long ago. In those days the people were hungry. No buffalo nor antelope were seen on the prairie. The deer and the elk trails were covered with grass and leaves; not even a rabbit could be found in the brush. Then the people prayed, saying: "Oh, Old Man, help us now, or we shall die. The buffalo and deer are gone. Uselessly we kindle the morning fires; useless are our arrows; our knives stick fast in the sheaths."

Then Old Man started out to find the game, and he took with him a young man, the son of a chief. For many days they travelled the prairies and ate nothing but berries and roots. One day they climbed a high ridge, and when they had reached the top, they saw, far off by a stream, a single lodge.

"What kind of a person can it be," said the young man, "who camps there all alone, far from friends?"

"That," said Old Man, "is the one who has hidden all the buffalo and deer from the people. He has a wife and a little son."

Then they went close to the lodge, and Old Man changed himself into a little dog, and he said, "That is I." Then the young man changed himself into a root-digger, 1 and he said, "That is I."

Now the little boy, playing about, found the dog, and he carried it to his father, saying, "Look! See what a pretty little dog I have found."

"Throw it away," said his father; "it is not a dog." And the little boy cried, but his father made him carry the dog away. Then the boy found the root-digger; and, again picking up the dog, he carried them both to the lodge, saying, "Look, mother! see the pretty root-digger I have found!"

"Throw them both away," said his father; "that is not a stick, that is not a dog."

"I want that stick," said the woman; "let our son have the little dog."

"Very well," said her husband, "but remember, if trouble comes, you bring it on yourself and on our son." Then he sent his wife and son off to pick berries; and when they were out of sight, he went out and killed a buffalo cow, and brought the meat into the lodge and covered it up, and the bones, skin and offal he threw in the creek. When his wife returned, he gave her some of the meat to roast; and while they were eating, the little boy fed the dog three times, and when he gave it more, his father took the meat away, saying, "That is not a dog, you shall not feed it more."

In the night, when all were asleep, Old Man and the young man arose in their right shapes, and ate of the meat. "You were right," said the young man; "this is surely the person who has hidden the buffalo from us." "Wait," said Old Man; and when they had finished eating, they changed themselves back into the stick and the dog.

In the morning the man sent his wife and son to dig roots, and the woman took the stick with her. The dog followed the little boy. Now, as they travelled along in search of roots, they came near a cave, and at its mouth stood a buffalo cow. Then the dog ran into the cave, and the stick, slipping from the woman's hand, followed, gliding along like a snake. In this cave they found all the buffalo and other game, and they began to drive them out; and soon the prairie was covered with buffalo and deer. Never before were seen so many.

Pretty soon the man came running up, and he said to his wife, "Who now drives out my animals?" and she replied, "The dog and the stick are now in there." "Did I not tell you," Said he, "that those were not what they looked like? See now the trouble you have brought upon us," and he put an arrow on his bow and waited for them to come out. But they were cunning, for when the last animal—a big bull— was about to go out, the stick grasped him by the hair under his neck, and coiled up in it, and the dog held on by the hair beneath, until they were far out on the prairie, when they changed into their true shapes, and drove the buffalo toward camp.

When the people saw the buffalo coming, they drove a big band of them to the pis´kun; but just as the leaders were about to jump off, a raven came and flapped its wings in front of them and croaked, and they turned off another way. Every time a band of buffalo was driven near the pis´kun, this raven frightened them away. Then Old Man knew that the raven was the one who had kept the buffalo cached.

So, he went and changed himself into a beaver, and lay stretched out on the bank of the river, as if dead; and the raven, which was very hungry, flew down and began to pick at him. Then Old Man caught it by the legs and ran with it to camp, and all the chiefs came together to decide what should be done with it. Some said to kill it, but Old Man said, "No! I will punish it," and he tied it over the lodge, right in the smoke hole.

As the days went by, the raven grew poor and weak, and his eyes were blurred with the thick smoke, and he cried continually to Old Man to pity him. One day Old Man untied him, and told him to take his right shape, saying: "Why have you tried to fool Old Man? Look at me! I cannot die. Look at me! Of all peoples and tribes, I am the chief. I cannot die. I made the mountains. They are standing yet. I made the prairies and the rocks. You see them yet. Go home, then, to your wife and your child, and when you are hungry hunt like any one else, or you shall die."

How the Old Man, Made People

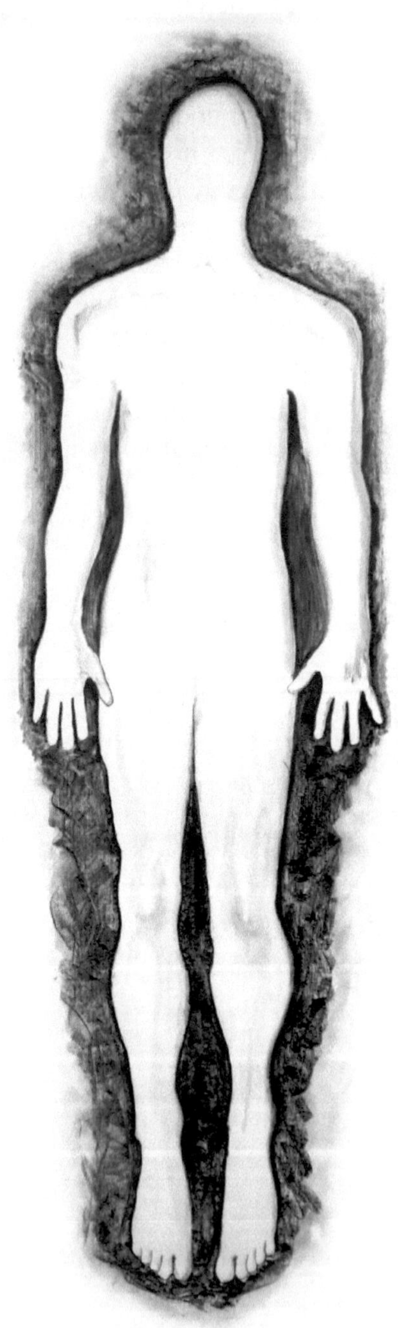

Long ago, when the world was new, there was no one living in it at all, except the Old Man, Na-pe, and his sometimes-friend and sometimes-enemy A-pe'si, the Coyote, and a few buffalo. There were no other people and no other animals. But the Old Man changed all that. He changed it first because he was lonely, and then because he was lazy; and maybe be shouldn't have, but anyway, he did. And this was the way of it.

Na-pe was sitting by his fire one day, trying to think of some way to amuse himself. He had plenty to eat--a whole young buffalo; no need to go hunting. He had a lodge; no work to do; and a fire. He was comfortable, but he wasn't contented. His only companion, A-pe'si the Coyote, was off somewhere on some scheme of his own, and anyway he had quarreled with A-pe'si, and they were on bad terms; so even if he had been there, Old Man would still have been lonely. He poked some sticks in the fire, threw a rock or two in the river, lit his pipe, and walked around. . . then sat down, and thought how nice it would be to have someone to smoke with, and to talk to. "Another one, like me," he thought. And he poked some more sticks in the fire, and threw some more rocks in the river.

Then he thought, "Why not? I am the Old Man! I can make anything I want to. Why shouldn't I make another like me, and have a companion?" And he promptly went to work.

First, he found a little still pool of water, and looked at his reflection carefully, so as to know just what he wanted to make. Then he counted his bones as best he could, and felt the shape of them.

Next, he went and got some clay, modelled a lot of bones, and baked them in his fire. When they were all baked, he took them out and looked at them. Some of them were very good, but others were crooked, or too thin, or had broken in the baking. These he put aside in a little heap.

Then he began to assemble the best of the clay bones into a figure of a man. He tied them all together with buffalo sinews, and smoothed them all carefully with buffalo fat. He padded them with clay mixed with buffalo blood, and stretched over the whole thing skin taken from the inside of the buffalo. Then he sat down and lit his pipe again.

He looked at the man he had made rather critically. It wasn't exactly what he had wanted, but still it was better than nothing.

"I will make some more," said Na-pe.

He picked the new man up and blew smoke into his eyes, nose, and mouth, and the figure came to life. Na-pe sat him down by the fire, and handed him the pipe. Then he went to get more clay.

All day long Na-pe worked, making men. It took a long time, because some of the bones in each lot weren't good, and he must discard them and make others. But at last, he got several men, all sitting by the fire and passing the pipe around. Na-pe sat down with them, and was very happy. He left the heap of discarded bones where they were, at the doorway of his lodge.

So, Na-pe and the men lived in his camp, and the men learned to hunt, and Na-pe had company, someone to smoke with, and they were all quite contented.

But the heap of left-over bones was a nuisance. Every time one of the men went in or out of Na-pe's lodge, they tripped over the bones. The wind blew through them at night, making a dreadful noise. The bones frequently tumbled over, making more of a disturbance. Na-pe intended to throw them in the river, but he was a bit lazy, and never got around to it. So, the left-over bones stayed where they were.

By this time A-pe'si, the Coyote, was back from wherever he had been. He went around the camp, looking the men over, and being very superior, saying that he didn't think much of Na-pe's handiwork. He was also critical of the heap of bones at the door of the lodge. "I should think you would do something with them--make them into men," said A-pe'si, the Coyote.

"All right, I will," said Na-pe. "Only they aren't very good. It will be difficult to make men out of them!" "Oh, I'll help, I'll help!" said A-pe'si. "With my cleverness, we will make something much better than these poor creatures of yours!" So, the two of them set to work. The discarded bones, clicking and tattling, were sorted out, and tied together. Then Na-pe mixed the clay and the buffalo blood to cover them. He fully intended to make the bones into men, but A-pe'si the Coyote kept interfering; consequently, when the job was done, the finished product was quite different. Na-pe surveyed it dubiously, but he blew the smoke into its eyes and nose and mouth, as he had with the men. And the woman came to life.

A-pe'si and Na-pe made the rest of the bones into women, and as they finished each one, they put them all together, and the women immediately began to talk to each other. A-pe'si was very pleased with what he had done. "When I made my men," said Na-pe, "I set them down by the fire to smoke."

And even to this day, if you have one group of men, and another of women, the men will want to sit by the fire and smoke. But the women talk. And whether it is because they were made out of the left-over bones that clicked and rattled, or whether it is because A-pe'si, the Coyote --who is a noisy creature himself--had a part in their making, no one can say.

The Badger and the Bear

Lakota Legend

On the edge of a forest there lived a large family of badgers. In the ground their dwelling was made. Its walls and roof were covered with rocks and straw. Old father badger was a great hunter. He knew well how to track the deer and buffalo.

Every day he came home carrying on his back some wild game. This kept mother badger very busy, and the baby badgers very chubby. While the well-fed children played about, digging little make-believe dwellings, their mother hung thin sliced meats upon long willow racks. As fast as the meats were dried and seasoned by sun and wind, she packed them carefully away in a large thick bag.

This bag was like a huge stiff envelope, but far more beautiful to see, for it was painted all over with many bright colors. These firmly tied bags of dried meat were laid upon the rocks in the walls of the dwelling. In this way they were both useful and decorative. One day father badger did not go off for a hunt. He stayed at home, making new arrows. His children sat about him on the ground floor.

Their small black eyes danced with delight as they watched the gay colors painted upon the arrows. All of a sudden there was heard a heavy footfall near the entrance way. The oval-shaped door-frame was pushed aside. In stepped a large black foot with great big claws. Then the other clumsy foot came next. All the while the baby badgers stared hard at the unexpected comer. After the second foot, in peeped the head of a big black bear!

His black nose was dry and parched. Silently he entered the dwelling and sat down on the ground by the doorway. His black eyes never left the painted bags on the rocky walls. He guessed what was in them. He was a very hungry bear. Seeing the racks of red meat hanging in the yard, he had come to visit the badger family.

Though he was a stranger and his strong paws and jaws frightened the small badgers, the father said, "Hau, how, friend! Your lips and nose look feverish and hungry. Will you eat with us?"

"Yes, my friend," said the bear. "I am starved. I saw your racks of red fresh meat, and knowing your heart is kind, I came hither. Give me meat to eat, my friend."

Hereupon the mother badger took long strides across the room, and as she had to pass in front of the strange visitor, she said: "Ah han! Allow me to pass!" which was an apology.

"Hau, hau!" replied the bear, drawing himself closer to the wall and crossing his shins together.

Mother badger chose the most tender red meat, and soon over a bed of coals she broiled the venison.

That day the bear had all he could eat. At nightfall he rose, and smacking his lips together (that is the noisy way of saying "the food was very good!") he left the badger dwelling. The baby badgers, peeping through the door-flap after the shaggy bear, saw him disappear into the woods near-by.

Day after day the crackling of twigs in the forest told of heavy footsteps. Out would come the shame black bear. He never lifted the door-flap, but thrusting it aside entered slowly in. Always in the same place by the entrance way he sat down with crossed shins. His daily visits were so regular that mother badger placed a fur rug in his place. She did not wish a guest in her dwelling to sit upon the bare hard ground.

At last, one time when the bear returned, his nose was bright and black. His coat was glossy. He had grown fat upon the badger's hospitality. As he entered the dwelling a pair of wicked gleams shot out of his shaggy head.

Surprised by the strange behavior of the guest who remained standing upon the rug, leaning his round back against the wall, father badger queried, "Hau, my friend! What?"

The bear took one stride forward and shook his paw in the badger's face. He said: "I am strong, very strong!"

"Yes, yes, so you are," replied the badger. From the farther end of the room mother badger muttered over her bead work: "Yes, you grew strong from our well-filled bowls."

The bear smiled, showing a row of large sharp teeth. "I have no dwelling. I have no bags of dried meat. I have no arrows. All these I have found here on this spot," said he, stamping his heavy foot. "I want them! See! I am strong!" repeated he, lifting both his terrible paws.

Quietly the father badger spoke, "I fed you. I called you friend, though you came here a stranger and a beggar. For the sake of my little ones leave us in peace."

Mother badger, in her excited way, had pierced hard through the buckskin and stuck her fingers repeatedly with her sharp awl until she had laid aside her work. Now, while her husband was talking to the bear, she motioned with her hands to the children. On tiptoe they hastened to her side.

For reply came a low growl. It grew louder and more fierce. "Wa-ough!" he roared, and by force hurled the badgers out. First the father badger; then the mother. The little badgers he tossed by pairs. He threw them hard upon the ground.

Standing in the entranceway and showing his ugly teeth, he snarled, "Be gone!" The father and mother badger, having gained their feet, picked up their kicking little babes, and, wailing aloud, drew the air into their flattened lungs till they could stand alone upon their feet. No sooner had the baby badgers caught their breath than they howled and shrieked with pain and fright. Ah! what a dismal cry was theirs as the whole badger family went forth wailing from out their own dwelling!

A little distance away from their stolen house the father badger built a small round hut. He made it of bent willows and covered it with dry grass and twigs. This was shelter for the night; but alas! it was empty of food and arrows. All day father badger prowled through the forest, but without his arrows he could not get food for his children. Upon his return, the cry of the little ones for meat, the shad quiet of the mother with bowed head, hurt him like a poisoned arrow wound. "I'll beg meat for you!" said he in an unsteady voice.

Covering his head and entire body in a long loose robe he halted beside the big black bear. The bear was slicing red meat to hang upon the rack. He did not pause for a look at the comer. As the badger stood there unrecognized, he saw that the bear had brought with him his whole family. Little cubs played under the high-hanging new meats. They laughed and pointed with their wee noses upward at the thin sliced meats upon the poles.

"Have you no heart, Black Bear? My children are starving. Give me a small piece of meat for them," begged the badger.

"Wa-ough!" growled the angry bear, and pounced upon the badger. "Be gone!" said he, and with his big hind foot he sent father badger sprawling on the ground. All the little ruffian bears hooted and shouted "ha-ha!" to see the beggar fall upon his face.

There was one, however, who did not even smile. He was the youngest cub. His fur coat was not as black and glossy as those his elders wore. The hair was dry and dingy. It looked much more like kinky wool. He was the ugly cub.

Poor little baby bear! He had always been laughed at by his older brothers. He could not help being himself. He could not change the differences between himself and his brothers. Thus again, though the rest laughed aloud at the badger's fall, he did not see the joke. His face was long and earnest. In his heart he was shad to see the badgers crying and starving. In his breast spread a burning desire to share his food with them. "I shall not ask my father for meat to give away. He would say 'No!' Then my brothers would laugh at me," said the ugly baby bear to himself.

In an instant, as if his good intention had passed from him, he was singing happily and skipping around his father at work. Singing in his small high voice and dragging his feet in long strides after him, as if a prankish spirit oozed out from his heels, he strayed off through the tall grass. He was ambling toward the small round hut.

When directly in front of the entranceway, he made a quick side kick with his left hind leg. Lo! there fell into the badger's hut a piece of fresh meat. It was tough meat, full of sinews, yet it was the only piece he could take without his father's notice. Thus, having given meat to the hungry badgers, the ugly baby bear ran quickly away to his father again.

On the following day the father badger came back once more. He stood watching the big bear cutting thin slices of meat. "Give..." he began, when the bear turning upon him with a growl, thrust him cruelly aside.

The badger fell on his hands. He fell where the grass was wet with the blood of the newly carved buffalo. His keen starving eyes caught sight of a little red clot lying bright upon the green. Looking fearfully toward the bear and seeing his head was turned away, he snatched up the small thick blood.

Underneath his girdled blanket he hid it in his hand. On his return to his family, he said within himself: "I'll pray the Great Spirit to bless it."

Thus, he built a small round lodge. Sprinkling water upon the heated heap of sacred stones within, he made ready to purge his body. "The buffalo blood, too, must be purified before I ask a blessing upon it," thought the badger.

He carried it into the sacred vapor lodge. After placing it near the sacred stones, he sat down beside it. After a long silence, he muttered: "Great Spirit, bless this little buffalo blood." Then he arose, and with a quiet dignity stepped out of the lodge.

Close behind him some one followed. The badger turned to look over his shoulder and to his great joy he beheld a Lakota brave in handsome buckskins. In his hand he carried a magic arrow. Across his back dangled a long-fringed quiver.

In answer to the badger's prayer, the avenger had sprung from out the red globules.

"My son!" exclaimed the badger with extended right hand.

"Hau, father," replied the brave; "I am your avenger!"

Immediately the badger told the sad story of his hungry little ones and the stingy bear. Listening closely the young man stood looking steadily upon the ground. At length the father badger moved away. "Where?" queried the avenger.

"My son, we have no food. I am going again to beg for meat," answered the badger.

"Then I go with you," replied the young brave. This made the old badger happy. He was proud of his son. He was delighted to be called "father" by the first human creature.

The bear saw the badger coming in the distance. He narrowed his eyes at the tall stranger walking beside him. He spied the arrow. At once he guessed it was the avenger of whom he had heard long, long ago.

As they approached, the bear stood erect with a hand on his thigh. He smiled upon them. "How, badger, my friend! Here is my knife. Cut your favorite pieces from the deer," said he, holding out a long thin blade.

"Hau!" said the badger eagerly. He wondered what had inspired the big bear to such a generous deed.

The young avenger waited till the badger took the long knife in his hand. Gazing full into the black bear's face, he said: "I come to do justice. You have returned only a knife to my poor father. Now return to him his dwelling."

His voice was deep and powerful. In his black eyes burned a steady fire. The long strong teeth of the bear rattled against each other, and his shaggy body shook with fear.

"Ahow!" cried he, as if he had been shot. Running into the dwelling he gasped, breathless and trembling, "Come out, all of you! This is the badger's dwelling. We must flee to the forest for fear of the avenger who carries the magic arrow."

Out they hurried, all the bears, and disappeared into the woods. Singing and laughing, the badgers returned to their own dwelling.

Then the avenger left them. "I go," said he in parting, "over the Earth."

The Bear and the Rabbit Hunt Buffalo

Once upon a time there lived as neighbors, a bear and a rabbit. The rabbit was a good shot, and the bear being very clumsy could not use the arrow to good advantage. The bear was very unkind to the rabbit. Every morning, the bear would call over to the rabbit and say: "Take your bow and arrows and come with me to the other side of the hill. A large herd of buffalo are grazing there, and I want you to shoot some of them for me, as my children are crying for meat."

The rabbit, fearing to arouse the bear's anger by refusing, consented, and went with the bear, and shot enough buffalo to satisfy the hungry family. Indeed, he shot and killed so many that there was lots of meat left after the bear and his family had loaded themselves, and packed all they could carry home. The bear being very gluttonous, and not wanting the rabbit to get any of the meat, said: "Rabbit, you come along home with us and we will return and get the remainder of the meat."

The poor rabbit could not even taste the blood from the butchering, as the bear would throw earth on the blood and dry it up. Poor Rabbit would have to go home hungry after his hard day's work.

The bear was the father of five children. The youngest boy was very kind to the rabbit. The mother bear, knowing that her youngest was a very hearty eater, always gave him an extra-large piece of meat. What the baby bear did not eat, he would take outside with him and pretend to play ball with it, kicking it toward the rabbit's house, and when he got close to the door, he would give the meat such a great kick, that it would fly into the rabbit's house, and in this way poor Rabbit would get his meal unknown to the papa bear.

Baby bear never forgot his friend Rabbit. Papa bear often wondered why his baby would go outside after each meal. He grew suspicious and asked the baby where he had been. "Oh, I always play ball outside, around the house, and when I get tired playing, I eat up my meat ball and then come in."

The baby bear was too cunning to let papa bear know that he was keeping his friend rabbit from starving to death. Nevertheless, papa bear suspected baby and said: "Baby, I think you go over to the rabbit's after every meal."

The four older brothers were very handsome, but baby bear was a little puny fellow, whose coat couldn't keep out much cold, as it was short and shaggy, and of a dirty brown color. The three older brothers were very unkind to baby bear, but the fourth one always took baby's part, and was always kind to his baby brother.

Rabbit was getting tired of being ordered and bullied around by papa bear. He puzzled his brain to scheme some way of getting even with Mr. Bear for abusing him so much. He studied all night long, but no scheme worth trying presented itself. Early one morning Mr. Bear presented himself at Rabbit's door.

"Say, Rabbit, my meat is all used up, and there is a fine herd of buffalo grazing on the hillside. Get your bow and arrows and come with me. I want you to shoot some of them for me."

"Very well," said Rabbit, and he went and killed six buffalo for Bear. Bear got busy butchering and poor Rabbit, thinking he would get a chance to lick up one mouthful of blood, stayed very close to the bear while he was cutting up the meat. The bear was very watchful lest the rabbit get something to eat. Despite bear's watchfulness, a small clot of blood rolled past and behind the bear's feet. At once Rabbit seized the clot and hid it in his bosom. By the time Rabbit got home, the blood clot was hardened from the warmth of his body, so, being hungry, it put Mr. Rabbit out of sorts to think that after all his trouble he could not eat the blood.

Very badly disappointed, he lay down on his floor and gazed up into the chimney hole. Disgusted with the way things had turned out, he grabbed up the blood clot and threw it up through the hole. Scarcely had it hit the ground when he heard the voice of a baby crying, "Ate! Ate!" (father, father). He went outside and there he found a big baby boy. He took the baby into his house and threw him out through the hole again. This time the boy was large enough to say "Ate, Ate, he-cun-sin-lo." (Father, father, don't do that). But nevertheless, he threw him up and out again. On going out the third time, there stood a handsome youth smiling at him. Rabbit at once adopted the youth and took him into his house, seating him in the seat of honor (which is directly opposite the entrance), and saying: "My son, I want you to be a good, honest, straightforward man. Now, I have in my possession a fine outfit, and you, my son, shall wear it."

Suiting his action to his words, he drew out a bag from a hollow tree and on opening it, drew out a fine buckskin shirt (tanned white as snow), worked with porcupine quills. Also, a pair of red leggings worked with beads. Moccasins worked with colored hair. A fine otter skin robe. White weasel skins to intertwine with his beautiful long black locks. A magnificent center eagle feather. A rawhide covered bow, accompanied by a quiver full of flint arrowheads.

The rabbit, having dressed his son in all the latest finery, sat back and gazed long and lovingly at his handsome son. Instinctively Rabbit felt that his son had been sent him for the purpose of being instrumental in the downfall of Mr. Bear. Events will show.

The morning following the arrival of Rabbit's son, Mr. Bear again presents himself at the door, crying out: "You lazy, ugly rabbit, get up and come out here. I want you to shoot some more buffalo for me."

"Who is this, who speaks so insultingly to you, father?" asked the son.

"It is a bear who lives near here, and makes me kill buffalo for his family, and he won't let me take even one little drop of blood from the killing, and consequently, my son, I have nothing in my house for you to eat."

The young man was anxious to meet Mr. Bear but Rabbit advised him to wait a little until he and Bear had gone to the hunt. So, the son obeyed, and when he thought it time that the killing was done, he started out and arrived on the scene just as Mr. Bear was about to proceed with his butchering.

Seeing a strange shadow on the ground beside him, Mr. Bear looked up and gazed into the fearless eyes of rabbit's handsome son.

"Who is this?" asked Mr. Bear of poor little Rabbit.

"I don't know," answered Rabbit.

"Who are you?" asked the bear of Rabbit's son. "Where did you come from?"

The rabbit's son not replying, the bear spoke thus to him: "Get out of here, and get out quick, too."

At this speech the rabbit's son became angered, and fastened an arrow to his bow and drove the arrow through the bear's heart. Then he turned on Mrs. Bear and served her likewise. During the melee, Rabbit shouted: "My son, my son, don't kill the two youngest. The baby has kept me from starving and the other one is good and kind to his baby brother."

So, the three older brothers who were unkind to their baby brother met a similar fate to that of their selfish parents.

This (the story goes) is the reason that bears travel only in pairs.

Race with Buffalo

Cheyenne
A story of the Cheyenne of the Great Plains

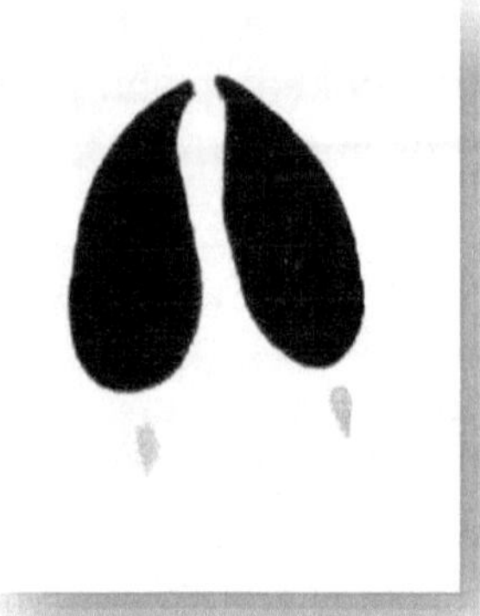

There was a time when all the animals lived in peace, when no one ate anyone else. All the animals were the same color, because they had not yet painted their faces.

Buffalo was the largest and strongest of the animals, and he was getting hungry, He wanted to be the chief of all the animals. He wanted to draw strength from all the other animals by eating their flesh. Buffalo wanted to become the eater of all the animals.

The Human People also said that they should become the chief of all the animals. People wanted to draw strength from all the other animals by eating their flesh. People wanted to become the eaters of all the other animals.

Buffalo challenged the Human People to a race; the winner of the race would become the chief of all the animals. The People said that they would accept such a challenge, but since buffaloes have four legs and People have only two, the People claimed the right to have another animal run the race in the People's place. The buffaloes consented.

The People chose the Bird People to represent them in the race. They chose Hummingbird, Meadowlark, Hawk, and Magpie. All the other animals and birds wanted to join the race, too, each of them thinking that just maybe they too had a chance to become chief of all the animals. All the animals took paint and painted the faces for the race, each according to his or her spiritual vision.

Skunk painted a white strip on himself and his symbol for the race. Antelope painted himself the color of the earth for the race. Raccoon painted black circles around his eyes and around his tail. Robin painted herself brown with a red breastplate.

The race was to be held at the edge of the Black Hills at the place known as Buffalo Gap. The competitors would race from the starting line sticks to the turn around stick and then back to the starting line. All the animals, painted according to their vision, lined up between the sticks. Among the animals were the Bird People, who would run the race with their wings for the Human People, and Runs Slender Buffalo, the fastest runner of all the buffaloes.

The cry was given to begin and all the animals and birds set out on the race. Hummingbird took the lead, ahead of Runs Slender Buffalo, but his wings were so small that he soon fell behind. As the animals neared the turn around stick, Runs Slender Buffalo took the lead. Then Meadowlark came up beside Runs Slender Buffalo, and the two went along side by side right into the turn. Runs Slender Buffalo wheeled around the stick, her hooves thundering, and she pulled away from Meadowlark, who went wide to make the turn.

The animals in the lead passed the late runners who were still headed for the stick. Meadowlark fell behind and cheered on Hawk as he passed her. Hawk gained on Run Slender Buffalo, and it looked like he might pass her. Her heart was pounding and her legs were tiring. But Hawk's wings were tiring also, and he soon fell behind.

Runs Slender Buffalo was nearing the finish line as the winner. It looked like the Buffalo People would become the eaters of all the animals!

Then, behind the buffalo woman, wings beating steadily, came Magpie. She was not a quick starter, but her wing beats were hard and true. Her heart was strong. Her eyes did not wander form the finish line. She never looked back. Her wings were wide and she drove herself forward with beat after beat after beat. All the other animals had fallen behind. Runs Slender Buffalo looked over at the magpie, but the magpie never looked away from the starting sticks.

With each beat of her wings, she moved past Runs Slender Buffalo by no more than the length of her bill. At the starting sticks, many animals began to line up to watch the finish. Raccoon, who had fallen out of the race early, had returned to the starting sticks. Now he stood up between the sticks and put out his little hands for the runners to touch as they passed. He would feel the touch of whoever was in the lead, and turn toward the winner.

Closer and closer came Runs Slender Buffalo, and some of the animals feared Raccoon would be trampled. Magpie gradually flew nearer to the ground so she could brush Raccoon's little hands as she flew past. Raccoon did not move, but stared straight at the onrushing pair. Magpie seemed to be pulling ahead. Runs Slender Buffalo leaned forward as she ran to touch Raccoon's hand with her great nose.

Magpie's wingtip touched Raccoon's little hand and he turned toward her and instant before Runs Slender Buffalo thundered past and he was surrounded by a great cloud of dust. All the animals waited breathlessly for the dust to settle. At last, there stood Raccoon with his little hand raised toward the path of Magpie.

The Human People had won the race!

The Buffalo wandered the Great Plains and ate grass and the people became the great hunters, the chief of all animals.

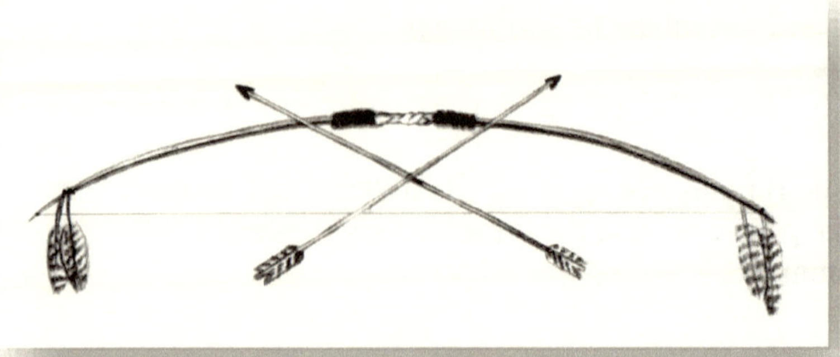

The Life And Death Of Sweet Medicine

Northern Cheyenne

A long time ago the people had no laws, no rules of behavior - they hardly knew enough to survive. And they did shameful things out of ignorance, because they didn't understand how to live.

There was one man among them who had a natural sense of what was right. He and his wife were good, hard-working people, a family to be proud of. They knew how to feel ashamed, and this feeling kept them from doing wrong.

Their only child was a daughter, beautiful and modest, who had reached the age when girls begin to think about husbands and making a family. One night a man's voice spoke to her in a dream: "You are handsome and strong, modest and young. Therefore, Sweet Root will visit you."

Dismissing it as just a dream, the girl went cheerfully about her chores the next day. On the following night, however, she heard the voice again: "Sweet Root is coming - woman's medicine which makes a mother's milk flow. Sweet Root is coming as a man comes courting."

The girl puzzled over the words when she awoke, but in the end shrugged her shoulders. People can't control their dreams, she thought, and the idea of a visit from a medicine root didn't make sense.

On the third night the dream recurred, and this time it was so real that a figure seemed to be standing beside the buffalo robe she slept on. He was talking to her, telling her: "Sweet Root is coming; he is very near. Soon he will be with you."

On the fourth night she heard the same voice and saw the same figure. Disturbed, she told her mother about it the next morning. "There must be something in it," she said. It's so real, and the voice is so much like a man's voice."

"No, it's just a dream," said her mother. "It doesn't mean anything."

But from that time on, the girl felt different. Something was stirring, growing within her, and after a few months her condition became obvious: she was going to have a baby.

She told her parents that no man had touched her, and they believed her. But others would not be likely to, and the girl hid her condition. When she felt the birth pangs coming on, she went out into the prairie far from the camp and built herself a brush shelter.

Doing everything herself, she gave birth to a baby boy. She dried the baby, wrapped him in soft moss, and left him there in the wickiup, for in her village a baby without a father would be scorned and treated badly. Praying that someone would find him, she went sadly home to her parents.

At about the same time, an old woman was out searching the prairie for wild turnips, which she dug up with an animal's shoulder blade. She heard crying, and following the sound, came to the wickiup. She was overjoyed to find the baby, as she had never had one of her own. All around the brush shelter grew the sweet root which makes a mother's milk flow, so she named the boy Sweet Medicine. She took him home to her shabby tipi even though she had nothing to offer him but love.

In the tipi next to the old woman's lived a young mother who was nursing a small child, and she agreed to nurse Sweet Medicine also. He grew faster and learned faster than ordinary children and was weaned in no time. When he was only ten years old, he already had grown-up wisdom and hunting skill far in advance of his age. But because he had no family and lived at the edge of the camp in a poor tipi, nobody paid any attention to Sweet Medicine's exceptional powers.

That year there was a drought, very little game, and much hunger in the village. "Grandmother," Sweet Medicine said to the old woman, "find me an old buffalo hide - any dried-out, chewed-up scrap with holes in it will do."

The woman searched among the refuse piles and found a wrinkled, brittle piece that the starving dogs had been chewing on. When she brought it to Sweet Medicine, he told her, "Take this to the stream outside the camp, wash it in the flowing water, make it pliable, scrape it clean." After she had done this Sweet Medicine took a willow wand and bent it into a hoop, which he colored with sacred red earth paint. He cut the buffalo hide into one long strip and wove it back and forth over the hoop, making a kind of net with an opening in the center. Then he cut four wild cherry sticks, sharpened them to a point, and hardened them in the hearth fire.

The next morning, he said: "Grandmother, come with me. We're going to play the hoop-and-stick game." He took the hoop and the cherry-wood sticks and walked into the middle of the camp circle. "Grandmother, roll this hoop for me," he said. She rolled the hoop along the ground and Sweet Medicine hurled his pointed sticks through the center of it, hitting the right spot every time. Soon a lot of people, men and women, boys and girls, came to watch the strange new game.

Then Sweet Medicine cried: "Grandmother, let me hit it once more and make the hoop into a fat buffalo calf!"

Again, he threw his stick like a dart, again the stick went through the center of the hoop, and as it did so the hoop turned into a fat, yellow buffalo calf. The stick had pierced its heart, and the calf fell down dead. "Now you people will have plenty to eat," said Sweet Medicine. "Come and butcher this calf."

The people gathered and roasted chunks of tender calf meat over their fires. And no matter how many pieces of flesh they cut from the calf's body; it was never picked clean. However much they ate, there was always more. So, the people had their fill, and that was the end of the famine. It was also the first hoop-and-stick game played among the Cheyenne. This sacred game has much power attached to it, and it is still being played.

A boy's first kill is an important happening in his life, something he will always remember. After killing his first buffalo a boy will be honored by his father, who may hold a feast for him and give him a man's name. There would be no feast for Sweet Medicine; all the same, he was very happy when he killed a fat, yellow buffalo calf on his first hunt. He was skinning and butchering it when he was approached by an elderly man, a chief too old to do much hunting, but still harsh and commanding. "This is just the kind of hide I have been looking for," said the chief. I will take it."

"You can't have a boy's first hide," said Sweet Medicine. "Surely you must know this. But you are welcome to half of the meat, because I honor old age."

The chief took the meat but grabbed the hide too and began to walk off with it. Sweet Medicine took hold of one end, and they started a tug-of-war. The chief used his riding whip on Sweet Medicine, shouting: "How dare a poor nothing boy defy a chief?" As he whipped Sweet Medicine again and again across the face, the boy's fighting spirit was aroused. He grabbed a big buffalo leg bone and hit the old man over the head.

Some say Sweet Medicine killed that chief, others say the old man just fell down stunned. But in the village the people were angry that a mere boy had dared to fight the old chief. Some said, "Let's whip him," others said, "Let's kill him."

After he had returned to the old woman's lodge, Sweet Medicine sensed what was going on. He said: "Grandmother, some young men of the warrior societies will come here to kill me for having stood up for myself." He thanked her for her kindness to him and then fled from the village. Later when the young warriors came, they were so angry to find the boy gone that they pulled the lodge down and set fire to it.

The following morning someone saw Sweet Medicine, dressed like a Fox warrior, standing on a hill overlooking the village. His enemies set out in pursuit, but he was always just out of their reach and they finally retired exhausted. The next morning, he appeared as an Elk warrior, carrying a crooked coupstick wrapped in otter skin.

Again, they tried to catch and kill him, and again he evaded them. They resumed their futile chase on the third morning, when he wore the red face paint and feathers of a Red Shield warrior, and on the fourth, when he dressed like a Dog soldier and shook a small red rattle tied with buffalo hair at his pursuers. On the fifth day he appeared in the full regalia of a Cheyenne chief. That made the village warriors angrier than ever, but they still couldn't catch him, and after that they saw him no more.

Wandering alone over the prairie, the boy heard a voice calling, leading him to a beautiful dark-forested land of many hills. Standing apart from the others was a single mountain shaped like a huge tipi: the sacred medicine mountain called Bear Butte. Sweet Medicine found a secret opening which has since closed for perhaps was visible to him alone) and entered the mountain. It was hollow inside like a tipi, forming a sacred lodge filled with people who looked like ordinary men and women, but were really powerful spirits.

"Grandson, come in, we have been expecting you," the holy people said, and when Sweet Medicine took his seat, they began teaching him the Cheyenne way to live so that he could return to the people and give them this knowledge.

First of all, the spirits gave him the sacred four arrows, saying: "This is the great gift we are handing you. With these wonderful arrows, the tribe will prosper. Two arrows are for war and two for hunting. But there is much, much more to the four arrows. They have great powers. They contain rules by which men ought to live."

The spirit people taught Sweet Medicine how to pray to the arrows, how to keep them, how to renew them. They taught him the wise laws of the forty-four chiefs. They taught him how to set up rules for the warrior societies. They taught him how women should be honored. They taught him the many useful things by which people could live, survive, and prosper, things people had not yet learned at that time. Finally, they taught him how to make a special tipi in which the sacred arrows were to be kept. Sweet Medicine listened respectfully and learned well, and finally an old spirit man burned incense of sweet grass to purify both Sweet Medicine and the sacred arrow bundle. Then the Cheyenne boy put the holy bundle on his back and began the long journey home to his people.

During his absence there had been a famine in the land. The buffalo had gone into hiding, for they were angry that the people did not know how to live and were behaving badly. When Sweet Medicine arrived at the village, he found a group of tired and listless children, their ribs sticking out, who were playing with little buffalo figures they had made out of mud. Sweet Medicine immediately changed the figures into large chunks of juicy buffalo meat and fat. "Now there's enough for you to eat," he told the young ones, "with plenty left over for your parents and grandparents. Take the meat, fat, and tongues into the village, and tell two good young hunters to come out in the morning to meet me."

Though the children carried the message and two young hunters went out and looked everywhere for Sweet Medicine the next day, all they saw was a big eagle circling above them. They tried again on the second and third days with no success, but on the fourth morning they found Sweet Medicine standing on top of a hill overlooking the village. He told the two: "I have come bringing a wonderful gift from the Creator which the spirits inside the great medicine mountain have sent you. Tell the people to set up a big lodge in the center of the camp circle. Cover its door with sage, and purify it with burning sweet grass. Tell everyone to go inside the tipi and stay there; no one must see me approaching. "

When at last all was ready, Sweet Medicine walked slowly toward the village and four times called out: "People of the Cheyenne, with a great power I am approaching. Be joyful. The sacred arrows I am bringing." He entered the tipi with the sacred arrow bundle and said: "You have not yet learned how to live in the right way. That is why the Ones Above were angry and the buffalo went into hiding."

The two young hunters lit the fire, and Sweet Medicine filled a deer-bone pipe with sacred tobacco. All night through, he taught the people what the spirits inside the holy mountain had taught him. These teachings established the way of the Tsistsistas, the true Cheyenne nation.

Toward morning Sweet Medicine sang four sacred songs. After each song he smoked the pipe, and its holy breath ascended through the smoke hole up into the sky, up to the great mystery.

At daybreak, as the sun rose and the people emerged from the sacred arrow lodge, they found the prairie around them covered with buffalo. The spirits were no longer angry. The famine was over.

For many nights to come, Sweet Medicine instructed the people in the sacred laws. He lived among the Cheyenne for a long time and made them into a proud tribe respected throughout the Plains.

Four lives the Creator had given him, but even Sweet Medicine was not immortal. Only the rocks and mountains are forever. When he grew old and feeble and felt that the end of his appointed time was near, he directed the people to carry him to a place near the Sacred Bear Butte. There they made a small hut for him out of cottonwood branches and cedar lodge poles covered with bark and leaves. They spread its door with sage, flat cedar leaves, and fragrant grass. It was a good lodge to die in, and when they placed him before it, he addressed the people for the last time:

I have seen in my mind that some time after I am dead - and may the time be long - light-skinned, bearded men will arrive with sticks spitting fire. They will conquer the land and drive you before them. They will kill the animals who give their flesh that you may live, and they will bring strange animals for you to ride and eat. They will introduce war and evil, strange sicknesses and death. They will try to make you forget Maheo, the Creator, and the things I taught you, and will impose their own alien, evil ways. They will take your land little by little, until there is nothing left for you. I do not like to tell you this, but you must know. You must be strong when that bad time comes, you men, and particularly you women, because much depends on you, because you are the perpetuators of life and if you weaken, the Cheyenne will cease to be. Now I have said all there is to say.

Then Sweet Medicine went into his hut to die.

-Told by members of the Strange Owl family on the Lame Deer Indian Reservation, Montana, 1967, and recorded by Richard Erdoes.

Origin of the Sacred Arrow

A Gros Ventre Legend

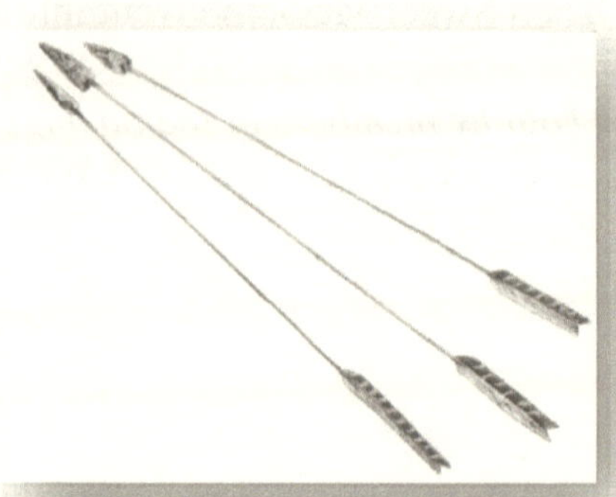

Charred Body had his origin in the skies. There was a big village up there and this man was a great hunter. He used to go out and bring in Buffalo, Elk, Antelope until the Buffalo became scarce - they scattered out far from the village. So, one day he told his close relatives, "The Buffalo seem to have gone far away from here, and I am tired of hunting them so long. Some day they may multiply again, but now I am going to build a mound to sit on and look over the country." He made a practice of going up to his mound at intervals of three or four days to survey the land and listen to its sounds. One day toward nightfall he heard Buffalo bellowing. He was excited. He could not tell from what direction the sound came. He was in the habit of changing himself into an arrow shot from a bow and thus making in one day a journey such as a man would ordinarily make in ten days. The next day he went out to the mound, changed himself into an arrow, and went into every direction, but found no Buffalo. Back on the mound he again heard the Buffalo, and they seemed so close that he thought it strange he could not place them. The next day when he went out to the mound he took an arrow and stuck it into the ground, and as the ground opened up a crack, he worked the hole. There below he saw Buffalo as if the Chokeberries are half ripe, and the bulls were fighting and bellowing. This was the sound he had heard.

He went back to his lodge and told his relatives that he had seen the Buffalo, thousands upon thousands, but since, if he went down below, it would be difficult to pack the meat back, he decided to go down ahead and build a dwelling and his brothers and sisters-in-law should follow afterwards. They could themselves see by looking down the hole that there would be Buffalo enough for all.

The chief of the village was named Long Arm. He was regarded as a holy man. He usually knew what was going on from day to day. Charred Body told him of the land he had found, so beautiful and plentiful in game. Charred Body said, "I want to leave this place and go down there, but it will not be possible to pack the meat back up here or to drive the Buffalo up here from the Earth. So I shall go down there to live and take with me all those near relatives of mine who are bound to me like a thread of the Spider web, and we shall make our home there." Long Arm said neither yes nor no; he uttered no word. The hunter went back to the hole, transformed himself into an arrow and flew through the air to Earth.

He came down so swiftly that as he landed on the ground the arrow struck the Earth, and it seemed as if he were stuck there for good. The place where he landed was near Washburn by a creek some People call Turtle, but which we call Charred Body Creek. There was an evil spirit in the creek whose moccasin tops were like a flame of fire so that when he went through the forest the Cottonwood Trees would burn down. He would undo the flap of the moccasin when he went to Windward and wave it back and forth over the ground; when he tied it up again the flame ceased. This man feared the man from Heaven lest he establish villages or take away his land or even kill him, so he caused a Windstorm and set the Prairie on fire and the flames charred the arrow here and there. Hence the name "Charred

Body" is derived. Since the arrow could not pull himself out, he decided to make a spring; thus, he loosened himself. So, he decreed that the spring would flow as long as the World would last; you can see even today where the spring is.

Charred Body established thirteen lodges, First, he looked about and found a good site and established one lodge, then another, until he had thirteen built. Then he went back into the heavens and told what had happened and how the old man with flame about the foot had tried to kill him, how he had found the spring and how good the game was. He made it sound so attractive. He said that he went by the arrow and hence could take down only as many families as there were parts to the arrow. He would take his nearest relatives only, with their children. The groove at the end of the arrow to put the string into was one lodge. The three feathers were regarded as lodges; that made four. The two sinews bound about it were two others, making six. The three points of the arrowhead were three other lodges, making nine. The three grooves circling around the arrow in a spiral made twelve. The arrow itself was the thirteenth; there were thirteen lodges all told. The spiral is considered as Lightning; hence the arrows power. If it does not come into contact with a bone, it will penetrate the Buffalo right through.

He called his nearest relatives and embraced them, and in embracing them he gave them the power of the arrow and encouraged them to follow him. First, he went down, then all came after and he assigned them lodges. When they first came down, the mysterious bodies down there knew that he was also mysterious and tried to kill him, but when he pulled himself out (of the hole made by the arrow point) they knew that they had no power against him. Before coming down, the People had made preparations and they brought seeds of corn, beans and so forth and began to plant corn on the ground by the river and to build scaffolds for drying the corn the meat. So, they lived happily for a long time. You can see today the remains of their thirteen villages, but obscured by high water and the ploughing farmers. I have heard that People have found arrowheads in the thirteen villages.

After a number of years, First Creator happened to come to the village. He asked some boys playing outside who was chief. They showed him the way to the large lodge in the center which was Charred Body's lodge. He asked Charred Body how he came there and Charred Body told him. He said it was well and that he wished to make friends with Charred Body; when there were two, they could talk matters over and act more effectively (than one), three were even better, but two were strong. They must therefore love one another. So, they became friends, ate and talked together, and First Creator stayed in the lodge several nights before he went on again.

When he came back, he reported that there was a big village East of them whose chief had a beautiful daughter. It was the custom in that village afternoon for the maidens to go along a wide path to the river for water and for the men to line up along the path and do their courting. The married women would go along the path outside the row. When a young girl came opposite a man who like her, he would clear his throat and if the girl liked him, it was a good sign. The next day he would ask a drink, and if she gave him a drink it was a better sign. So, People took notice, and if a girl gave a man a drink it became a matter of gossip, the parents came together to find out whether the two were industrious and able to run a household, and if everything was favorable, they were married. Now the chief's daughter had a strong will and never looked at the young men. When they tried to catch her eye, she paid them no attention. "Now, my friend," said First Creator, "You are handsome, not too slender, too tall or too short. Your hair is long and beautiful. No one could find a blemish upon you. You would certainly make a hit with the girl, so let's go over and try our luck. If you can get her and be a son-in-law to a great chief, you will be a renowned man."

So, it was agreed, and when they came to the edge of the village to a place where the moles had dug up a mound of earth, they began to dress themselves up. Charred Body mixed the dirt with water and daubed mud across his chin from ear to ear and upon his cheeks, brought his hair together in a big pompadour in front and stuck a plume in at the place where he tied it up. This feather the wind waved to and fro. His robe he wore open with his bow and arrows inside. Today we say of a person who combs his hair to the side in a pompadour that "he wears his hair like Charred Body."

They went to a certain lodge in the village and were kindly received. When First Creator told them who Charred Body was, they said, "We have heard about him and how he had a beautiful land in the skies and liked the country down here." When he said that they had come courting, the People said, "It is well." They went down to the path by the river and stood opposite each other and Coyote, which is another name for First Creator, said he would give a signal when the chief's daughter came so that his friend would pay no attention to the others. She came dressed in tanned white Deerskin with a robe of Elkskin from which the hair had been scraped, light and pliable as a plume. Charred Body stepped in front of her and she swerved. He turned also and she swerved again. When he was almost in front of her, he said, "I wish to drink out of your cup." She said, "What you have done is not according to our custom; you should not have moved from the line but just cleared your throat, and I shall give you no drink!" "Do you make those streaks across your face in imitation of the charring?" He was angry, took out his bow and arrows and, as she turned to flee, shot her twice in the back and killed her. A tumult arose and the two visitors fled back to the village.

Coyote warned Charred Body that he had done an evil deed and that this would not be the end of it. The chief was not likely to sit still and do nothing. He had owned the land before Charred Body came there, and Charred Body must therefore build barricades and protect himself. Charred Body paid little attention to him. "I go by the arrow and it can pierce through them." he said. "Even then, "said Coyote, "You are often out hunting, and while you are away, they may send out scouts and kill all in the village. More than one village may combine against you. You may think that you can fight them single-handed, but you have done a bad deed and this will cause your mind to stray, and while it is occupied with other things, they will overcome you. So, whatever you do, don't let anything distract your attention or you may be destroyed."

Day after day, Charred Body would go and sit on top of a hill where he had a mound and look over in the direction of the village where he had committed the crime. He told the young men to cut up sticks for arrows and sort them out into bundles and put them under his bed. When they came back, the sticks would be already made into arrows. Soon all the young men were supplied. But he was always in deep thought, first because of the crime he had committed and second lest the village come against him. One day Coyote offered to go over the village and find out what they were planning. He said that it would take corn-balls and pemmican and spread them on the outskirts of the village, and if anyone was wounded, he would give him the food and tell him it was Good Medicine for wounds. He would pretend that he had left Charred Body because of his crime. He met them on the way in such numbers as completely to surround the village. All who had children remained. When he had passed them, on the other side of the hill, he saw Meadowlark and sent him on an errand to fly to Charred Body on his mound and tell him to prepare four barricades as a great force was coming against him to avenge his crime.

Meadowlark carried the message, but as soon as Charred Body got back to the village to prepare the barricades, he forgot all about it. The enemy employed a Holy Man to make him forgetful; the Holy Man raised his hand against him and Charred Body forgot what was to happen. Three times Coyote sent Meadowlark with the message, and three times Charred Body forgot it as soon as he reached the village. The fourth time Meadowlark told him to make some sign on his body to attract attention. Charred Body stuck a bunch of grass in his hair and went back to the village. Again, he forgot the message. He went back to the lodge, but his head itched; he told his wife to scratch his head, and she found the grass and said. "This is the cause of your itching!" He gave a groan and sent word to the People that the next day the enemy would come against them; they must prepare a barricade, get arrows ready and be brave even to death. He went out and cut Bog Brush, put them under his bed and commanded it to turn to June Bushes. When he took it out, it had become June Bush, and he peeled the bark and made more arrows.

Coyote (in the enemy's camp) said, "You have been sending out scouts but their reports are not clear. I will go myself to see what is going on." He started on a run, fell with his foot out of joint, and claimed it was too painful to put in again and that he was now too disabled to fight with them in the attack against the village. He said, "Way down on the river they are performing rites for Medicine, so I will go there and bring back corn-balls and pemmican." He caused an announcement to be sounded at a distance (He must been a ventriloquist) which said; "All you who have Medicine Bags and Mysteries, come and join in this ceremony to be performed."

He told them that he had an adopted son in the enemy's camp who was Mysterious in battle. He could not be shot by an arrow and they must keep away from him. "You will find him dressed with a bladder covering his head daubed with white clay. His body will have streaks lengthwise and crosswise. His quiver is a Coyote's hide. He will wound many of you, but I will bring a hide for the wounded to lie on and feed them corn-balls and pemmican." As soon as he was out of sight, he threw away his crutch, set his foot again, turned into a Coyote and ran around another way into the village and became a man again. He asked after Charred Body and learned that he was making arrows. But a weasel had just been in to see Charred Body, and it had scattered and trampled arrows. Charred Body had been angry and struck four times at the weasel; the fourth time it ran out and Charred Body after it. "I told him whatever happened, not allow anything to distract him!" said Coyote. "But never mind, I am here. Don't turn into women!" Charred Body's sister was at this time with child, and Coyote told her to go inside a celler-hole, and he would cover her over so that she would not be burned.

When the battle took place, there were four among the enemy's band who had supernatural power. One had no head, but only a big mouth from shoulder to shoulder into which he sucked his enemies; another was an old woman with a basket which whenever she turned, sucked in people or birds of the air; a third was the man with the flaming moccasins; a fourth was a beaver (called Tail-With-A-Knife) whose tail was sharp both sides. These four helped the enemy. Tail-With-A-Knife chopped down the barricade, Flame-Around-His-Ankle encircled the village and set it on fire. Coyote was in the thick of the battle dressed as he had described. When he saw that all was lost, he disappeared in a cloud of smoke.

Meanwhile, Charred Body was still chasing Yellow Weasel. It seems that there was a transformation of the Earth so that Charred Body found himself far to the North. Yellow Weasel said "Look back and see your own village!" He looked and saw the smoke. He wanted to get back as quickly as possible. His eyesight would be too slow, for he would have to stop at the end of each sight, so he used his thinking power, transformed himself into thought, and wished himself back to his village. There he found the place in flames.

Now after the battle, the enemy had withdrawn and were relating their exploits. It seemed to them as if Coyote had fought in the battle, and Coyote heard their word as he came limping back with the hide, corn-balls and pemmican. An old bear was appointed to discover whether Coyote had been in the battle. The way he did this was to lift up his paw and put it on a person, then put his paw to his nose and smell it. When Coyote entered, the paw was raise to test him, but Coyote put a corn-ball into the paw, saying, "You greedy fellow, you want this all to yourself!" then he had the wounded brought in and laid upon the robe, and gave them corn-ball and pemmican. He said, "However wounded you may be yourselves, you have destroyed the village and enticed Charred Body away." And he said, "These People were just like relatives to me, and I want to go back there and walk through the place where young men and maidens formally walked, and think about their sports and laughter and mourn there for them." So, they consented and he went on his way.

Close to the village he saw Charred Body walking among the dead. As was the custom in those days, Coyote walked up to him, put his arm about his neck, and wept over him. Then he told him where he had hidden the sister, and they went to the cellar to see if she were alive. When they lifted up the hide, she came out, but when she saw the desolation of the village she wept and the men with her. Coyote proposed that they have a lodge, to live in together. He faced the North, raised both eyes, and he said, "I wish for a lodge facing South furnished with bedding and all things necessary and with a scaffold in front." When they opened their eyes, there it stood just like Coyote had said. There was no food, so Coyote said, "There is all kinds of food on the hoof; let us go out and see what we can take." They followed up the creek and killed Buffalo, cut it up, left the backbone, head and shoulders and took the best pieces. The kidney, back-gut and liver they washed to be eaten raw. These raw parts are considered a tonic today to keep one from sickness. The woman at the lodge cooked for them. She began to slice the meat and roast the ribs close to the fire and they felt themselves at home once more.

After they had lived thus from day to day, bringing in game until there was plenty, Coyote went away to the enemy's camp to see what the People were doing, promising to return again. It is an old custom with both Mandan and Gros Ventre that when a sister is alone in the house, a brother must not enter out of respect to his sister. Only if someone else is with her is it right for him to enter. Hence Charred Body did not think it was right to stay alone with his sister, so he went off hunting by day to bring in his choice bits of food for her and told his sister on no account to let anyone into the house if anyone should come round asking for at the door. "No one can come in if you do not take out the crossbar," he said. One day when he came back from hunting, he saw his sister outside looking as if she were laughing, and he took the meat and waited for her, but she did not come in.

This is what happened...........

While he was away on the hunt, she had heard a voice crying, "Tuk, tuk, tuk! my daughter, where can the door be?" She forgot that her brother had told her and undid the door for the stranger. There entered a headless monster. He said, "Place me on the West side between the pillows." She said, "Grandfather, what will you have to eat?" He said, "The best is the fat of the stomach. When I eat this fat I must have a pregnant woman lie on her back and then I place the hot fat upon her and eat in this way." The woman was frightened and only half cooked it. He held it himself to the fire, and the flames wrapped his hands but he did not seem to feel it. He made her lie down on the floor and place the hot fat upon her. The woman screamed and twins were born and the woman died. The monster took one by the leg and threw it into the center of the lodge and said, "Lodge center, make this boy your slave!" The other he threw into the spring and said, "Spring, take this child for yours!" Then he took the door-posts which forked and set them outside and place the woman against them and held out her lips with two sticks as if she were laughing. Then he gathered up all the food and was gone.

When Charred Body knew that his sister was dead, he made a burial scaffold for her and by means of a crude lattice he placed her body upon it and cried bitterly. In the evening he came home and was preparing an evening meal when he heard a wee voice from the center of the lodge say, "Brother, give me something to eat." Twice this happened; then he investigated. He cut up a splinter and wrapped fat into it and, using a torch, he looked into the dark spot from which the voice came and found a baby boy. He brought the child to his knee. This was the child who called him "brother"

When Coyote drifted back, he found to his amazement that their sister had been killed, and he mourned her loss. One day he said, "Can't we do something for our brother here? Let us take this baby up and wish that he grow to a certain height." This is the song that Charred Body sang: First he took sweet grass and smoked him; then he raised him up and sang, "I want my child to grow high!" Coyote did the same. Charred Body raised him again and sang and he became a boy of twelve. Coyote got up and raised him and sang, "I want my brother to be the height of a man," and he became like a boy of eighteen. And at the same time, since the boys were twins, the Spring-Boy attended the same height also.

Since the boy was now grown, he was left to look after the lodge when the two went hunting, and every time this happened, Spring-Boy came out and played with him. The name of the Lodge-Boy was A-tu-tish, which means, "Near-the-edge-of-the-lodge" and Spring-Boy was Ma-hash from Ma-ha, meaning "Spring" He was dark and his brother was light and a little taller than Spring-Boy. The two men kept Buffalo tongues strung up and wondered why they disappeared so rapidly. "Are there two of you?" they asked, but the boy denied it. They had to bite the tongue, and compared the mark left by Spring-Boy's teeth, and they were different. At last, Lodge-Boy confessed that he had known all the time what happened when his mother was killed by the stranger and he was taken by the leg and given to the edge of the wall as a slave, and his brother had been thrown into the spring. The brother did not recall this. Spring-Boy seems to have been a kind of maverick - he did not belong to anyone. He had a long tusk and lived on water creatures and was influenced by his wild life in the spring. If anyone tried to catch him, he would tear him to pieces with his tusk. They arranged a plan to catch him. The boys used to play with gambling sticks and a round stone with a hole bored through. The men fixed up two Buffalo hides as a kind of armor with a lace down the back to hold it tight. In the game there was to be a dispute, and when the boy got down on his knees to look and see if the ring lay on the stick, Lodge-Boy was to jump on his back, tangle up his hair and thrust a stick to which a bladder was fastened. If he ran for the spring, they would catch him by the bladder. They then prepared a sweat lodge with hot stones and water ready, and transformed themselves into arrowheads. Spring-Boy came trotting up, quick and agile, and encircled the lodge to see if there was anyone about. He complained of smelling his brother, but Lodge-Boy told him that was because they had been there before going out hunting. He came into the lodge and was surprised to see the bladder; Lodge-Boy told him it was used to separate the marrow from the bones. He asked about the sweat-bath and was told it was for the men when they came home from hunting. They began to play, and when Spring-Boy knelt down to see how the ring had fallen, Lodge-Boy jumped upon him, wound his legs about his body, and the two boys rolled on the ground, and Spring-Boy's tusk could be heard snapping at his brother. The two men dashed in, dragged him to the sweat-bath and began to switch him, crying, "What kind of a person are you? You are a human being and you should behave like one." Spring-Boy cried out, "I am coming to myself!" They drew him out and examined his mouth, but the tusk still showed. Three times they returned him to the bath and poured water and switched his flesh; the fourth time the tusk disappeared and he lay exhausted. So, they fastened up his hair and thrust a stick through it, to which the bladder was attached. The moment he was released he ran to the spring and jumped in, but was unable to go under because of the bladder. After the fourth time of trying to get under water, he surrendered. They gave him water to drink, inserted two fingers into his mouth, and he vomited up all the water creatures which he had eaten and was restored to the ways of the men.

Now there were four occupants of the lodge. Several days passed before Spring-Boy came entirely to his senses. The men he was accustomed to call, "Your brothers" and one day he said, "I wish you would tell your brothers to make bow and arrows, two painted red and two black for me and the same for you." Lodge-Boy said, "You always talk indirectly to our brothers, but we are twins. We are from the Sky. There is a big village where we came from. The chief is Long-Arm and he knows everything that is going on and is called a Holy Man. When our brother Charred Body wanted to come down here to this Earth, he asked permission, and although Long-Arm said neither yes nor no, he took it upon himself to come down here, and this had led to the destruction of all our relatives. But the Holy Man knows what is going on below there. Our brother and Coyote went courting and our brother killed the chief's daughter. So, there was a fight, but our brother Coyote stowed our mother away in a cellar, and I knew all these things that were going on. One of the formidable men who took part in the fight was a monster with no head but a big mouth from shoulder to shoulder who lives around the bend of the creek. He killed our mother, and I knew all about it and thought that you did too." Spring-Boy said that through living in the spring, he had forgotten all these things. The arrows he had asked for the men made for the boys. Then they went through a ceremonial and Spring-Boy said that these arrows, one painted black and one red for each boy, were to be kept sacred and used in an emergency, and they were to have other arrows for daily use.

One day as they walked near their mother's grave, Spring-Boy proposed that they use the sacred arrows to bring their mother to life. The two brothers had watched the arrow rite. When the two hunters had gone out before sunrise, they took down the arrows from the quiver, burned sweet grass and sang the arrow song. They did the same for the bow, resting one end of the bow on Buffalo bull manure while they strung it. Then they went out where their mother lay. Spring-Boy placed one arrow in position, sang the arrow song and let it fly. They could see it go up into the sky like a streak of flame. As it fell the boys cried, "Mother! Mother! Look out! The arrow is going to hit you!" The figure began to move. Spring-Boy sent the third arrow, and this time mother sat up. Lodge-Boy shot the fourth arrow and the mother yawned and stretched her arms. She said, "I must have slept a long time; I feel tired." The boy set up a ladder to the scaffold and the mother came down to embrace them and said, "My spirit remained here and was about to return to my People when you sent the arrow. You are motherless and it is a joy that you have done this for me and my spirit has returned to my body." When they returned to the lodge, she noticed at once how the meat was cut in strings, not in the nice flat pieces that a woman is accustomed to cut. So, she ate a hearty meal. In time came Charred Body and Coyote home from hunting, and as Charred Body threw down his pack, he recognized his sister and they all cried for joy, and she told him how her spirit had pitied the children and had lingered about until it had been restored to her body by means of the sacred arrows.

Charred Body warned the boys that although they had more supernatural power than he did, they must never lie down to take a nap without setting four arrows in the ground, one at each of the four directions, and lying within the arrows with the head resting to the North or to the West (for even the ordinary person should never rest his head South or to the East) and they must place their moccasins to point to the West, not toward the East, because all spirits go to the East. Among Mandan and Gros Ventre, a dead person is always placed with the head to the East.

On day the boys went out to survey the country and they came to an old man who they knew to be Flame-Around-The-Ankle. They stood side-by-side and asked him to give them a demonstration of his power. He loosened the strings of his moccasin, let the flap fall, and they saw flames leaping. They asked him to run about a cottonwood tree; he trotted about the tree; he trotted about it in a circle and the tree fell over in flames. Spring-Boy asked to try the moccasin. "Surely you may!" He ran about a tree, then back to his brother, and then all at once he circled the old man and burned him to ashes. Then the boys ran shouting and laughing home to their mother pretending that Flames was chasing them.

Again, the boys wandered out, and as they followed up the creek, Lodge-Boy said, "Brother, right in that dense timber on the side of the hill lives the monster without a head who carried his mouth on his shoulders. Let us go over and have a look at him!" They approached cautiously; then turning into Chickadees, they flew over the monster's den and, perching on a tree, began to call. They filled a water bag made out of a Buffalo paunch and had a heated stone red-hot and caused it to shrink so that they could carry it in the curve of a stick. They first got a big stone, then went into their Mysteries and rubbed it until it became small. To this day, when we heat a stone red-hot for the sweat-bath we call it "The Chickadees' stone." When the monster came out and opened his mouth to swallow them, they dropped the hot stone. As it went down his gullet, he thought, it must be their claws that scratch so! "Enlarge, enlarge!" called the boys to the stone. He snatched the water-bag to drink and they said, "Enlarge yourself and hold more water!" The water began to boil in his stomach and the monster burst. The boys burned up his lodge, skinned him and placed the skin on Spring-Boy and ran back to the lodge as if the monster were after them. Its body was black; it had two tails and claws like a wildcat's. The mother was so delighted with the victory that she danced with joy, so from that time they dance when one wins a victory, generally the women but sometimes both women and men.

There was another mysterious spot where an old woman sucked People into a basket hung upon a post. They asked her to demonstrate her power. The woman was afraid of them, knowing they had supernatural power. A flock of birds was passing; she waved her basket to and fro and then to the side, and brought down the birds into the basket. Spring-Boy asked her to let him try. He took the basket, waved it as the old woman had done, and drew the woman into the basket. Thus, he killed her. Great was the joy of their mother when he brought her home dead in the basket.

All those Mysterious beings lived in the vicinity of Turtle Creek, which the People called Charred Body Creek, just about a couple of miles from Washburn.

Some time later the boys heard about the Beaver-With-Tail-Like-A-Knife, who could tear open the Earth with a blow. Even today you can see where his tail struck the Earth; it looks something like a shell-hole. The Beaver had sharp ears, but the boys laid in wait for him and Lodge-Boy shot an arrow through his head as if it were a big pumpkin.

When the Beaver was dead, they cut off his tail and brought it home.

These were the beings who lived about Washburn and had allied themselves with the enemy. There might be others living at a distance, but those who lived near were all destroyed. So, their mother's brothers urged them to attempt no more such exploits, and the boys agreed that their mother's safety was now assured. The wished, however, to wander further into the country, so they told their mother not to worry if they did not return and took their leave.

While all this was going on down below, the People in the Sky became uneasy lest the boys who had killed so many Mysterious beings below come up to the Sky and kill them. So, they held a council and asked Long-Arm to bring Spring-Boy, who was dark and reckless, up into the Sky and put him to death. Long-Arm told them he saw nothing wrong with the boys and did not wish their death. They belonged to their own People. The father and mother had had hard treatment and they avenged themselves justly. But the People cried out all the more against Spring-Boy and Long-Arm accordingly used his magic power to throw the boys into a sleep in the moon. That is the origin of daytime napping. The boys grew sleepy and, remembering their brother's instruction, they set up the arrows and placed their moccasins Westward with the bow and arrow beside them and went to sleep. Sun cast his direct rays upon them, making them sleepy. Then Long-Arm reached down to Earth to where Spring-Boy lay and picked him up and carried him up into the air.

The People arranged for Spring-Boy's death. They dug a hole and the chief bade them set up a tree there with forked branches, but all feared to cut the tree lest Spring-Boy come out alive and destroy the one who cut it down. They tried to persuade the woman to cut it, but they said, "If you are afraid, how much more should we weak women fear!" Then the chief decreed that a hermaphrodite should cut the three on which Spring-Boy was to be hung. As soon as Long-Arm brought Spring-Boy up, the People rushed upon him and beat him until he was nearly dead. They had already prepared the form of death he was to die. A rawhide was stretched across the arms of the crotch and wound around the tree while it was wet; when dry it was much tighter. The boy's arms were lanced next to the bone and his feet through the cords and rawhide strips were run through and brought right around the tree so that they hung by wrists and feet. After he was securely tied, they raised the tree and set it forth into the hole. They had put an Antelope hide, tanned soft, about his waist so that it hung below the knee, this on account of the number of women present. Over the tree they erected a kind of bower, the cross-pieces of which were inserted into the rawhide at the top of the tree. The hole was covered in leaves. All this time the boy said nothing, but now he spoke: "I have been delivered into your hands and I do not think evil of you, for my mother was one of you and I do not wish to destroy you. If this were done by an enemy it would not be strange, but as you are my own People, it does not seem right for you to cause me this agony. But you need not fear me." The People did not answer; they could not accuse him of nothing. (Today they do not put up a man, but kill a Buffalo and cut a strip along the back leaving the tail and raise it as if the Buffalo were angry and on the other end they put the Buffalo skull without the horns and hang this up to represent the Buffalo. They set up a bower about it and gather up the earth into a ridge on the North side and stick bog bush into it, beginning at each end leaving a place vacant between. They use to leave this space so that when the boy died his body could be laid down. Today they lay there the sacred Weasel or other Animals used in the ceremony. To the ridge of the West side sits the Holy Man in a robe worn hair side out.)

For three days Spring-Boy hung on the tree, then he began to get weary. Now when Lodge-Boy awoke from sleep he could not see his twin brother, he was alarmed and, taking the shape of flaming arrow, he flew over the Earth even to both sides of the Ocean, calling the name of Spring-Boy and, finding nothing, he returned to the place from which his brother had vanished. There he lay looking up into the sky, when he saw a streak of light at the point where Spring-Boy had been taken through. Flying through the air he entered at the same place and saw that the land was empty where all the multitudes had flocked after Spring-Boy. So he changed himself into a little boy with shaggy, uncombed hair and a big belly, who was nevertheless old enough to talk, and followed the People to the field where they massed about the bower. At the edge of the field was a lodge in which an old woman was sitting. He asked her for food and the old woman adopted him as a grandson; he waited upon her and she was glad. All this time they could hear singing going on in the bower. He said, "Grandmother, what is going on there?" So, she related the whole story of Charred Body's descent to Earth and his crime and how the People feared the boys and especially Spring-Boy because he was dark of color and reckless and how they had cut a tree and what Spring-Boy had said about his own People destroying him. "This is the third day and night and tomorrow at noon they will place his body on the ridge of the bower," she said, and she told him how they danced in the morning, at noon and in the evening and sang ten songs in rotation, and how they could not stop dancing until the ten songs were sung or extend the dance beyond them. For a drum they used a long rawhide without hair which they beat with sticks, and the dancers whistled to the rhythm of the song. The best singers beat with sticks on four small round drums of wood covered with string on one side like a tambourine, which were to indicate the four nights of the dance. It was difficult to remember the order of the songs correctly. These four led the singing and the whole society must sing with the leader.

So, the little boy asked the women to take him to the bower. At the door she picked him up so that he could see and asked the People to make way for her and her grandchild. They were singing a song and dancing with whistles in their mouths and shouting to the man on the tree, "Be a man for one day more," As Spring-Boy looked about and saw his brother, a light shone about his head and he began to move and stretch as if he had been strengthened. Lodge-Boy, fearing he would be recognized, begged the old woman to take him outside. That evening they heard again the sound of songs and dancing. An announcer came through the village warning the young men and maidens not to sleep that night, but to keep watch lest Lodge-Boy come to his brother's rescue, for the Holy Man thought when he saw the light that Spring-Boy's brother must have come there to strengthen him. "My grandchild, did you hear what he was saying? He says Lodge-Boy is here!" said the grandmother. There she was, speaking to Lodge-Boy in person!

Rows of People slept at the bower to watch the place. When the old woman was snoring, the boy got up, took some Buffalo fat and went over to the place. Some slept, others were talking and moving about. It seemed impossible to reach his brother. He changed himself into a great Spider and crawled up to the post where his brother was. With the fat he greased his wounds, then he cut the thongs and the came down to the ground. There he found a stone hatchet with eyes, the very one used to cut the pole, and the Holy Man knew all about it but could do nothing because the two together were too powerful for him. Long-Arm went and placed his hand over the hole by which they passed through so as to catch them. Spring-Boy made a motion with the hatchet as if to cut it off the wrist and said, "This is the second time your hand has committed a crime, and it shall be a sign to the People on Earth." So, it is today that we see the hand in the heavens. Some People call it Orion. The belt is where they cut across the wrist: the thumb and fingers also show; they are hanging down like a hand. "The Hand Star" it is called.

The boys went back to the place where they had left the arrows sticking in the ground, pulled out the arrows, and went home to their mother. She told them that the People in the sky where like birds; they could fly about as they pleased. Since the opening was made in the heavens, they may come down to Earth. If a person lives well on Earth, his spirit takes flight to the skies and is able to come back again and be reborn, but if he is evil, he will wander about the Earth and never leave it for the skies. A baby born with a slit in the ear at the place where earrings are hung is such a reborn child from the People in the skies.

While the People sang and danced about Spring-Boy in the bower, he had ten songs learned and he instituted the ceremony on Earth in order to get power from the skies. In place of a man's body, he told them to use a Buffalo skin. They should hang themselves at the wrist and tied cords to their bodies and suspend the cords to the nose of the Buffalo skull and hang there just as he had been suspended. He said, "The person who performs the ceremony in memory of me may have the picture of the Sun on his chest and the half-moon on his back. The Sun causes things to grow and the moon causes the moisture. Since I have named the Buffalo hide as my own body, the Buffalo shall range where People are. In regard to the tree, the maidens of the village must be examined, and one who is a virgin shall cut down the tree and a young man, brave and unblemished, shall help her haul the tree to the dance place. In course of time, they shall marry and their seed multiply so that the People may live and not go out of existence."

The Gros Ventre (Hidatsa) People have believed in those rites. You can see where I have lanced across the chest in those ceremonies. They took hold of the flesh, lanced it through with a sharp knife and thrust a Juneberry stick cut about four inches long and wet with saliva through the lance-thrust and tied it with buckskin so that it would not slip off, then pushed back the chest. It hurt at first but not later. As I ran around (after being suspended to the tree) my feet would leave the Earth and I was suspended in air. Above my head I heard sounds like those made by Spirits and I believed them to be the Spirits of my helpers.

The chief celebrant at these ceremonies has usually killed an enemy. He cuts off the hand, brings it home, skins it, removes the bones and fills it with sand. After it dies, he empties out the sand and wears it at the back of the neck where it flaps up and down at the back and a white Antelope hide about his loins just as Spring-Boy wore it. Every night he uses the ridge of earth as a pillow. Since Spring-Boy hung on a tree for three days, and it took a fourth to escape back to the lodge, the ceremony lasts four days. The men lanced have to fast. The man who sleeps with his head on the ridge is naked and sage is strewn. The ceremony is called the Sundance in some tribes, but among the Hidatsa it is the "Hide-Beating"

The boys were worried for their mother's safety and the mother for that of the boys, so they sent the two older men and the mother to join the People in the sky and take back the hatchet and give it to the owner. The boys promised their mother to stay below and help the People on Earth in spirit as long as the world lasted and at the end of the world, she would see them again. The greasing of Spring-Boy's wounds by Lodge-Boy was the origin of the use of grease and tallow to heal wounds.

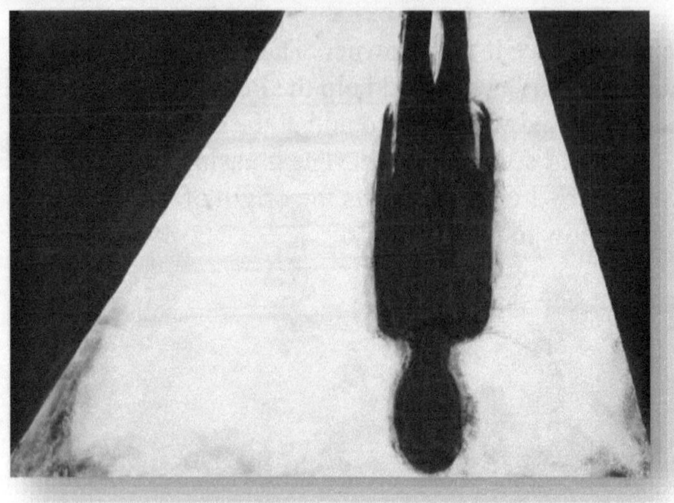

Deserted Children

A Gros Ventre Legend

There was a camp. All the children went off to play. They went to some distance. Then one man said, "Let us abandon the children. Lift the ends of your tent-poles and travois when you go, so that there will be no trail."

Then the people went off. After a time, the oldest girl amongst the children sent the others back to the camp to get something to eat. The children found the camp gone, the fires out, and only ashes about. They cried, and wandered about at random. The oldest girl said, "Let us go toward the river."

They found a trail leading across the river, and forded the river there. Then one of the girls found a tent-pole. As they went along, she cried, "My mother, here is your tent-pole." "Bring my tent-pole here!" shouted an old woman loudly from out of the timber. The children went towards her.

They found that she was an old woman who lived alone. They entered her tent. At night they were tired. The old woman told them all to sleep with their heads toward the fire. Only one little girl who had a small brother pretended to sleep, but did not. The old woman watched if all were asleep. Then she put her foot in the fire. It became red hot. Then she pressed it down on the throat of one of the children, and burned through the child's throat. Then she killed the next one and the next one.

The little girl jumped up, saying, "My grandmother, let me live with you and work for you. I will bring wood and water for you." Then the old woman allowed her and her little brother to live. "Take these out," she said.

Then the little girl, carrying her brother on her back, dragged out the bodies of the other children. Then the old woman sent her to get wood. The little girl brought back a load of cottonwood. When she brought it, the old woman said, "That is not the kind of wood I use. Throw it out. Bring another load." The little girl went out and got willow-wood. She came back, and said, "My grandmother, I have a load of wood." "Throw it in," said the old woman.

The little girl threw the wood into the tent. The old woman said, "That is not the kind of wood I use. Throw it outside. Now go get wood for me." Then the little girl brought birch-wood, then cherry, then sagebrush; but the old woman always said, "That is not the kind of wood I use," and sent her out again. The little girl went.

She cried and cried. Then a bird came to her and told her, " Bring her ghost- ropes for she is a ghost." Then the little girl brought some of these plants, which grow on willows. The old woman said, "Throw in the wood which you have brought." The little girl threw it in. Then the old woman was glad. "You are my good grand-daughter," she said.

Then the old woman sent the little girl to get water. The little girl brought her river-water, then rain-water, then spring-water; but the old woman always told her, "That is not the kind of water I use. Spill it!" Then the bird told the little girl, "Bring her foul, stagnant water, which is muddy and full of worms. That is the only kind she drinks." The little girl got the water, and when she brought it, the old woman was glad.

Then the little boy said that he needed to go out doors. "Well, then, go out with your brother, but let half of your robe remain inside of the tent while you hold him." Then the girl took her little brother out, leaving half of her robe inside the tent. When she was outside, she stuck an awl in the ground. She hung her robe on this, and, taking her little brother, fled.

The old woman called, "Hurry!" Then the awl answered, "My grandmother, my little brother is not yet ready." Again, the old woman said, "Now hurry!" Then the awl answered again, "My little brother is not ready." Then the old woman said, "Come in now; else I will go outside and kill you." She started to go out, and stepped on the awl.

The little girl and her brother fled, and came to a large river An animal with two horns lay there. It said, "Louse me." The little boy loused it. Its lice were frogs. "Catch four, and crack them with your teeth," said the Water-monster. The boy had on a necklace of plum-seeds. Four times the girl cracked a seed. She made the monster think that her brother had cracked one of its lice. Then the Water-monster said, "Go between my horns, and do not open your eyes until we have crossed." Then he went under the surface of the water.

He came up on the other side. The children got off and went on.

The old woman was pursuing the children, saying, "I will kill you. You cannot escape me by going to the sky or by entering the ground." She came to the river. The monster had returned, and was lying at the edge of the water. "Louse me," it said. The old woman found a frog. "These dirty lice! I will not put them into my mouth!" she said, and threw it into the river. She found three more, and threw them away. Then she went on the Water-monster. He went under the surface of the water, remained there, drowned her, and ate her. The children went on.

At last, they came to the camp of the people who had deserted them. They came to their parents' tent. "My mother, here is your little son," the girl said. "I did not know that I had a son," their mother said. They went to their father, their uncle, and their grandfather. They all said, "I did not know I had a son," "I did not know I had a nephew," "I did not know I had a grandson." Then a man said, "Let us tie them face to face, and hang them in a tree and leave them."

Then they tied them together, hung them in a tree, put out all the fires, and left them. A small dog with sores all over his body, his mouth, and his eyes, pretended to be sick and unable to move, and lay on the ground. He kept a little fire between his legs, and had hidden a knife. The people left the dog lying. When they had all gone off, the dog went to the children, climbed the tree, cut the ropes, and freed them. The little boy cried and cried. He felt bad about what the people had done.

Then many buffalo came near them. "Look at the buffalo, my brother," said the girl. The boy looked at the buffalo, and they fell dead. The girl wondered how they might cut them up. "Look at the meat, my younger brother," she said. The boy looked at the dead buffalo, and the meat was all cut up. Then she told him to look at the meat, and when he looked at it, the meat was dried. Then they had much to eat, and the dog became well again.

The girl sat down on the pile of buffalo-skins, and they were all dressed. She folded them together, sat on them, and there was a tent. Then she went out with the dog and looked for sticks. She brought dead branches, broken tent-poles, and rotten wood. "Look at the tent-poles," she said to her brother. When he looked, there were large straight tent-poles, smooth and good. Then the girl tied three together at the top, and stood them up, and told her brother to look at the tent.

He looked, and a large fine tent stood there. Then she told him to go inside and look about him. He went in and looked. Then the tent was filled with property, and there were beds for them, and a bed also for the dog. The dog was an old man. Then the girl said, "Look at the antelopes running, my brother." The boy looked, and the antelopes fell dead. He looked at them again, and the meat was cut up and the skins taken off.

Then the girl made fine dresses of the skins for her brother and herself and the dog. Then she called as if she were calling for dogs, and four bears came loping to her. "You watch that pile of meat, and you this one," she said to each one of the bears. The bears went to the meat and watched it. Then the boy looked at the woods and there was a corral full of fine painted horses. Then the children lived at this place, the same place where they had been tied and abandoned. They had very much food and much property.

Then a man came and saw their tent and the abundance they had, and went back and told the people. Then the people were told, "Break camp and move to the children for we are without food." Then they broke camp and traveled, and came to the children.

The women went to take meat, but the bears drove them away. The girl and her brother would not come out of the tent. Not even the dog would come out. Then the girl said, "I will go out and bring a wife for you, my brother, and for the dog, and a husband for myself."

Then she went out, and went to the camp and selected two pretty girls and one good-looking young man, and told them to come with her. She took them into the tent, and the girls sat down by the boy and the old man, and the man by her. Then they gave them fine clothing, and married them. Then the sister told her brother, "Go outside and look at the camp." The boy went out and looked at the people, and they all fell dead.

Why the Buffalo has a Hump

Adapted from G.E. Laidlaw, 1922, "Ojibwe Myths and Tales," Wisconsin Archeologist

Long ago, the Buffalo didn't have any hump. In the summer he would race across the prairies for fun, and the Foxes would run in front of him and tell all the little animals to get out of the way because the Buffalo was coming. They didn't know that Wenebojo was watching them.

So, the Buffalo raced across the prairies. There were little birds nesting on the ground and the Buffalo raced over them and tramped their nests. The little birds cried out and told him not to go near their nests, but Buffalo didn't listen to them and ran right over them.

The birds were sad and kept crying about their spoiled nests. Wenebojo heard them and he ran ahead of the Buffalo and Foxes and stopped them. With a stick, he hit the Buffalo on the shoulders, and the Buffalo hung his head and humped up his shoulders because he was afraid that Wenebojo would hit him with the stick again. But Wenebojo just said "You should be ashamed. You will always have a hump on your shoulder, and always carry your head low because of your shame." The Foxes were also afraid of Wenebojo and ran away and dug holes in the ground where they hid. And Wenebojo said to them "And you, Foxes, you will always live in the cold ground for hurting the birds." And that is why the Buffalo have humps, and why the Foxes have holes in the ground for their homes.

The Story of the Buffalo-painted Lodges

Blackfeet
"The Story of the Buffalo-painted Lodges" from "Blackfeet Indian Stories" by George Bird Grinnell 1913

The old lodges of the Piegans were made of buffalo skin and were painted with pictures of different kinds—birds, or animals, or trees, or mountains. It is believed that in most cases the first painter of any lodge was taught how he should paint it in a dream, but this was not always the case.

Two of the most important lodges in the Blackfeet camp are known as the Inis'kim lodges. Both are painted with figures of buffalo, one with black buffalo, and the other with yellow buffalo. Certain of the Inis'kim are kept in these lodges and can be kept in no others.

This story tells how these two lodges came to be made.

The painters were told what to do long, long ago, "in about the second generation after the first people."

In those days the old Piegans lived in the north, close to the Red Deer River. The camp moved, and the lodges were pitched on the river. One day two old men who were close friends had gone out from the camp to find some straight cherry shoots with which to make arrows. After they had gathered their 'shafts, they sat down on a high bank by the river and began to peel the bark from the shoots. The river was high. One of these men was named Weasel Heart and the other Fisher.

As they sat there, 'Weasel Heart chanced to look down into the water and saw something. He said to his comrade, "Friend, do you not see something down there where the water goes around?"

Fisher said, "No; I see nothing except buffalo," for he was looking across the river to the other side, and not down into the water.

"No," said Weasel Heart; "I do not mean over there on the prairie. Look down into that deep hole in the river, and you will see a lodge there."

Fisher looked as he had been told, and saw the lodge.

Weasel Heart said, "There is a lodge painted with black buffalo." As he spoke thus, Fisher said, "I see another lodge, standing in front of it." Weasel Heart saw that lodge too—the yellow-painted-buffalo lodge.

The two men wondered at this and could not understand how it could be, but they were both men of strong hearts, and presently Weasel Heart said, "Friend, I shall go down to enter that lodge. Do you sit here and tell me when I get to the place." Then Weasel Heart went up the river and found a drift-log to support him and pushed it out into the water, and floated down toward the cut bank. When he had reached the place where the lodge stood Fisher told him,

and he let go the log and dived down into the water and
entered the lodge.

In it he found two persons who owned the lodge, a man and
his wife. The man said to him, "You are welcome," and
Weasel Heart sat down. Then spoke the owner of the lodge
saying, "My son, this is my lodge, and I give it to you.
Look well at it inside and outside; and make your lodge
like this. If you do that, it may be a help to you."

Fisher sat a long time waiting for his friend, but at last he
looked down the stream and saw a man on the shore
walking toward him. He came along the bank until he had
reached his friend. It was Weasel Heart.

Fisher said to him, "I have been waiting a long time, and I
was afraid that something bad had happened to you."

Weasel Heart asked him, "Did you see me?"

"I saw you," said Fisher, "When you went into that lodge.
Did you, when you came out of the lodge, see there in the
water another lodge painted with yellow buffalo? Is it still
there?"

Weasel Heart said, "I saw it; it is there. Go you into the
water as I did."

Then Fisher went up the stream as his friend had gone and
entered the water at the same place and swam down as
Weasel Heart had done, and when Weasel Heart showed
him the place he dived down and disappeared as Weasel
Heart had disappeared. He entered the yellow painted-
buffalo lodge, and his friend saw him go into it.
In the lodge were two persons, a man and his wife. The
man said to him, "You are welcome; sit there." He spoke

further, saying, "My son, you have seen this lodge of mine; I give it to you. Look carefully at it, inside and outside, and fix up your lodge in that way. It may be a help to you hereafter." Then Fisher went out.

Weasel Heart waited for his friend as long as Fisher had waited for him, and when Fisher came out of the water it was at the place where Weasel Heart had come out. Then the two friends went home to the camp.

When the two had come to a hill near the camp they met a young man, and by him sent word that the people should make a sweat-house for them. After the sweat-house had been made, word was sent to them, and they entered the camp and went into the sweat-house and took a sweat, and all the time while they were sweating, sand was falling from their bodies.

Some time after that the people moved camp and went out and killed buffalo, and these two men made two lodges, and painted them just as the lodges were painted that they had seen in the river.

These two men had strong power which came to them from the Under-water People.

Once the people wished to cross the river, but the stream was deep and it was always hard for them to get across. Often the dogs and the travois were swept away and the people lost many of their things. At this time the tribe wished to cross, and Fisher and Weasel Heart said to each other, "The people want to cross the river, but it is high and they cannot do so. Let us try to make a crossing, so that it will be easier for them." So, Weasel Heart alone crossed the river and sat on the bank on the other side, and Fisher sat opposite to him on the bank where the camp was.

Then Fisher said to the people, "Pack up your things now and get ready to cross. I will make a place where you can cross easily."

Weasel Heart and Fisher filled their pipes and smoked, and then each started to cross the river. As each stepped into the water, the river began to go down, and the crossing grew more and more shallow. The people with all their dogs followed close behind Fisher, as he had told them to do. Fisher and Weasel Heart met in the middle of the river, and when they met, they stepped to one side up the stream and let the people pass them. Ever since that day this has been a shallow crossing.

These lodges came from the Under-water People—Su'ye-tup'pi. They were those who had owned them and who had been kind to Weasel Heart and Fisher.

The Blackfoot Genesis

Blackfoot Lodge Tales, George Bird Grinnell, [1892]

All animals of the Plains at one time heard and knew him, and all birds of the air heard and knew him. All things that he had made understood him, when he spoke to them, —the birds, the animals, and the people.

Old Man was travelling about, south of here, making the people. He came from the south, travelling north, making animals and birds as he passed along. He made the mountains, prairies, timber, and brush first. So, he went along, travelling northward, making things as he went, putting rivers here and there, and falls on them, putting red paint here and there in the ground, —fixing up the world as we see it to-day. He made the Milk River (the Teton) and crossed it, and, being tired, went up on a little hill and lay down to rest. As he lay on his back, stretched out on the ground, with arms extended, he marked himself out with stones, —the shape of his body, head, legs, arms, and everything. There you can see those rocks to-day. After he had rested, he went on northward, and stumbled over a knoll and fell down on his knees. Then he said, "You are a bad thing to be stumbling against"; so, he raised up two large buttes there, and named them the Knees, and they are called so to this day. He went on further north, and with some of the rocks he carried with him he built the Sweet Grass Hills.

Old Man covered the plains with grass for the animals to feed on. He marked off a piece of ground, and in it he made to grow all kinds of roots and berries, —camas, wild carrots, wild turnips, sweet-root, bitter-root, sarvis berries, bull berries, cherries, plums, and rosebuds. He put trees in the ground. He put all kinds of animals on the ground. When he made the bighorn with its big head and horns, he made it out on the prairie. It did not seem to travel easily on the prairie; it was awkward and could not go fast. So, he took it by one of its horns, and led it up into the mountains, and turned it loose; and it skipped about among the rocks, and went up fearful places with ease. So, he said, "This is the place that suits you; this is what you are fitted for, the rocks and the mountains." While he was in the mountains, he made the antelope out of dirt, and turned it loose, to see how it would go. It ran so fast that it fell over some rocks and hurt itself. He saw that this would not do, and took the antelope down on the prairie, and turned it loose; and it ran away fast and gracefully, and he said, "This is what you are suited to."

One day Old Man determined that he would make a woman and a child; so, he formed them both—the woman and the child, her son—of clay. After he had molded the clay in human shape, he said to the clay, "You must be people," and then he covered it up and left it, and went away. The next morning, he went to the place and took the covering off, and saw that the clay shapes had changed a little. The second morning there was still more change, and the third still more. The fourth morning he went to the place, took the covering off, looked at the images, and told them to rise and walk; and they did so. They walked down to the river with their Maker, and then he told them that his name was *Na'pi,* Old Man.

As they were standing by the river, the woman said to him, "How is it? will we always live, will there be no end to it?" He said: "I have never thought of that. We will have to decide it. I will take this buffalo chip and throw it in the river. If it floats, when people die, in four days they will become alive again; they will die for only four days. But if it sinks, there will be an end to them." He threw the chip into the river, and it floated. The woman turned and picked up a stone, and said: "No, I will throw this stone in the river; if it floats, we will always live, if it sinks people must die, that they may always be sorry for each other." The woman threw the stone into the water, and it sank. "There," said Old Man, "you have chosen. There will be an end to them."

It was not many nights after, that the woman's child died, and she cried a great deal for it. She said to Old Man: "Let us change this. The law that you first made, let that be a law." He said: "Not so. What is made law must be law. We will undo nothing that we have done. The child is dead, but it cannot be changed. People will have to die."

That is how we came to be people. It is he who made us.

The first people were poor and naked, and did not know how to get a living. Old Man showed them the roots and berries, and told them that they could eat them; that in a certain month of the year they could peel the bark off some trees and eat it, that it was good. He told the people that the animals should be their food, and gave them to the people, saying, "These are your herds." He said: "All these little animals that live in the ground—rats, squirrels, skunks, beavers—are good to eat. You need not fear to eat of their flesh." He made all the birds that fly, and told the people that there was no harm in their flesh, that it could be eaten. The first people that he created he used to take about through the timber and swamps and over the prairies, and show them the different plants. Of a certain plant he would say, "The root of this plant, if gathered in a certain month of the year, is good for a certain sickness." So, they learned the power of all herbs.

In those days there were buffalo. Now the people had no arms, but those black animals with long beards were armed; and once, as the people were moving about, the buffalo saw them, and ran after them, and hooked them, and killed and ate them. One day, as the Maker of the people was travelling over the country, he saw some of his children, that he had made, lying dead, torn to pieces and partly eaten by the buffalo. When he saw this, he was very sad. He said: "This will not do. I will change this. The people shall eat the buffalo."

He went to some of the people who were left, and said to them, "How is it that you people do nothing to these animals that are killing you?" The people said: "What can we do? We have no way to kill these animals, while they are armed and can kill us." Then said the Maker: "That is not hard. I will make you a weapon that will kill these animals." So, he went out, and cut some sarvis berry shoots, and brought them in, and peeled the bark off them. He took a larger piece of wood, and flattened it, and tied a string to it, and made a bow. Now, as he was the master of all birds and could do with them as he wished, he went out and caught one, and took feathers from its wing, and split them, and tied them to the shaft of wood. He tied four feathers along the shaft, and tried the arrow at a mark, and found that it did not fly well. He took these feathers off, and put on three; and when he tried it again, he found that it was good. He went out and began to break sharp pieces off the stones. He tried them, and found that the black flint stones made the best arrow points, and some white flints. Then he taught the people how to use these things.

Then he said: "The next time you go out, take these things with you, and use them as I tell you, and do not run from these animals. When they run at you, as soon as they get pretty close, shoot the arrows at them, as I have taught you;

and you will see that they will run from you or will run in a circle around you."

Now, as people became plenty, one day three men went out on to the plain to see the buffalo, but they had no arms. They saw the animals, but when the buffalo saw the men, they ran after them and killed two of them, but one got away. One day after this, the people went on a little hill to look about, and the buffalo saw them, and said, "*Saiyah*, there is some more of our food," and they rushed on them. This time the people did not run. They began to shoot at the buffalo with the bows and arrows *Na'pi* had given them, and the buffalo began to fall; but in the fight a person was killed.

At this time these people had flint knives given them, and they cut up the bodies of the dead buffalo. It is not healthful to eat the meat raw, so Old Man gathered soft dry rotten driftwood and made punk of it, and then got a piece of hard wood, and drilled a hole in it with an arrow point, and gave them a pointed piece of hard wood, and taught them how to make a fire with fire sticks, and to cook the flesh of these animals and eat it.

They got a kind of stone that was in the land, and then took another harder stone and worked one upon the other, and hollowed out the softer one, and made a kettle of it. This was the fashion of their dishes.

Also, Old Man said to the people: "Now, if you are overcome, you may go and sleep, and get power. Something will come to you in your dream, that will help you. Whatever these animals tell you to do, you must obey them, as they appear to you in your sleep. Be guided by them. If anybody wants help, if you are alone and travelling, and cry aloud for help, your prayer will be answered. It may be by the eagles, perhaps by the buffalo, or by the bears. Whatever animal answers your prayer, you must listen to him." That was how the first people got through the world, by the power of their dreams.

After this, Old Man kept on, travelling north. Many of the animals that he had made followed him as he went. The animals understood him when he spoke to them, and he used them as his servants. When he got to the north point of the Porcupine Mountains, there he made some more mud images of people, and blew breath upon them, and they became people. He made men and women. They asked him, "What are we to eat?" He made many images of clay, in the form of buffalo. Then he blew breath on these, and they stood up; and when he made signs to them, they started to run. Then he said to the people, "Those are your food." They said to him, "Well, now, we have those animals; how are we to kill them?" "I will show you," he said. He took them to the cliff, and made them build rock piles like this, >; and he made the people hide behind these piles of rock, and said, "When I lead the buffalo this way, as I bring them opposite to you, rise up."

After he had told them how to act, he started on toward a herd of buffalo. He began to call them, and the buffalo started to run toward him, and they followed him until they were inside the lines. Then he dropped back; and as the people rose up, the buffalo ran in a straight line and jumped over the cliff. He told the people to go and take the flesh of those animals. They tried to tear the limbs apart, but they could not. They tried to bite pieces out, and could not. So Old Man went to the edge of the cliff, and broke some pieces of stone with sharp edges, and told them to cut the flesh with these. When they had taken the skins from these animals, they set up some poles and put the hides on them, and so made a shelter to sleep under. There were some of

these buffalo that went over the cliff that were not dead.
Their legs were broken, but they were still alive. The
people cut strips of green hide, and tied stones in the
middle, and made large mauls, and broke in the skulls of
the buffalo, and killed them.

After he had taught those people these things, he started off
again, travelling north, until he came to where Bow and
Elbow rivers meet. There he made some more people, and
taught them the same things. From here he again went on
northward. When he had come nearly to the Red Deer's
River, he reached the hill where the Old Man sleeps. There
he lay down and rested himself. The form of his body is to
be seen there yet.

When he awoke from his sleep, he travelled further
northward and came to a fine high hill. He climbed to the
top of it, and there sat down to rest. He looked over the
country below him, and it pleased him. Before him the hill
was steep, and he said to himself, "Well, this is a fine place
for sliding; I will have some fun," and he began to slide
down the hill. The marks where he slid down are to be seen
yet, and the place is known to all people as the "Old Man's
Sliding Ground."

This is as far as the Blackfeet followed Old Man. The Crees
know what he did further north.

In later times once, *Na'pi* said, "Here I will mark you off a
piece of ground," and he did so. 1 Then he said: "There is
your land, and it is full of all kinds of animals, and many
things grow in this land. Let no other people come into it.
This is for you five tribes (Blackfeet, Bloods, Piegans, Gros
Ventres, Sarcees). When people come to cross the line, take
your bows and arrows, your lances and your battle axes,

and give them battle and keep them out. If they gain a footing, trouble will come to you."

Our forefathers gave battle to all people who came to cross these lines, and kept them out. Of late years we have let our friends, the white people, come in, and you know the result. We, his children, have failed to obey his laws.

About the Author

Thanks for choosing this book, if you enjoyed it, please leave positive feedback.

G.W. Mullins is an Author, Photographer, and Entrepreneur of Native American / Cherokee descent. He has been a published author for over 11 years. His writing has focused on the paranormal and Native American studies.

Mullins has released several books on the history/stories/fables of the Native American Indians. Among his books are the extremely successful "Star People, Sky Gods and Other Tales of the Native American Indians," "Story Teller An Anthology Of Folklore From The Native American Indians," "The Native American Story Book - Stories Of The American Indians For Children Volumes 1-5," "The Native American Cookbook," and "Walking With Spirits Native American Myths, Legends, And Folklore Volumes 1 Thru 6."

He has released the complete series of his Sci/fi Fantasy books "From The Dead Of Night," including the Best-Selling titles – "Daniel Is Waiting" and "Daniel Returns."

His most recent work includes the series "Rise Of The Snow Queen featuring Book One The Polar Bear King" and "Book Two War Of The Witches." Mullins' latest releases include two young adult fantasy series, "Rise of the Darklighter Book One: Dark Awakening" and the "Dream Walker" Book Series featuring "Enter the Sandman" & "Wide Awake In Dream Land." Among his other releases are "Messages from The Other Side" (a nonfiction book about communication with the dead), and the soon to be released "Convergence" (a post-apocalyptic book multi-series event coming in winter 2022).

For further information, on the writing, visit G.W. Mullins' web site at http://gwmullins.wix.com/books.

<u>Also Available From G.W. Mullins</u>

Daniel Awakens A Ghost Story Begins– From The Dead Of Night Prequel

Daniel Is Waiting A Ghost Story – From The Dead Of Night Book One

Daniel Returns A Ghost Story - From The Dead Of Night Book Two

Daniel's Fate – A Ghost Story Ends From The Dead Of Night Book Four

Rise Of The Snow Queen Book One The Polar Bear King

Messages From The Other Side Stories of the Dead, Their Communication, and Unfinished Business

Vengeance

Mysteries Of The Unseen World – Ghost, Hauntings and The Unexplained

Haunted America Stories Of Ghost, Hauntings And The Unexplained

Timeless – A Paranormal Romance Murder Mystery

Star People, Sky Gods, And Other Tales Of The Native American Indians

More Star People, Sky Gods, And Other Paranormal Tales Of The Native American Indians

Coyote Tales Of The Native American Indians

Bear Tales Of The Native American Indians

Walking With Spirits Native American Myths, Legends,
And Folklore Volumes One Thru Six

The Native American Cookbook

Native American Cooking - An Indian Cookbook With
Legends And Folklore

The Native American Story Book - Stories Of The
American Indians For Children Volumes One Thru Five

The Best Native American Stories For Children

Cherokee A Collection of American Indian Legends,
Stories And Fables

Creation Myths - Tales Of The Native American Indians

Strange Tales Of The Native American Indians

Spirit Quest - Stories Of The Native American Indians

Animal Tales Of The Native American Indians

Medicine Man - Shamanism, Natural Healing, Remedies
And Stories Of The Native American Indians

Native American Legends: Stories Of The Hopi Indians
Volumes One and Two

Totem Animals Of The Native Americans

The Best Native American Myths, Legends And Folklore
Volumes One Thru Three

Ghosts, Spirits And The Afterlife In Native American
Indian Mythology And Folklore

War Song: Tales Of The Native American Indians

Origin Tales Of The Native American Indians

Animal Tales Of The Native American Indians Vol. 2